Other Leisure Books by Romer Zane Grey featuring
characters created by Zane Grey:

YAQUI: SIEGE AT FORLORN RIVER

ARIZONA AMES: KING OF THE OUTLAW HORDE

BUCK DUANE: KING OF THE RANGE

LARAMIE NELSON: LAWLESS

NEVADA JIM LACY: BEYOND THE MOGOLLON RIM

ZANE GREY'S BUCK DUANE

THE RIDER
OF DISTANT TRAILS

Romer Zane Grey

Based on characters created by Zane Grey

LEISURE BOOKS   **NEW YORK CITY**

A LEISURE BOOK®

July, 1999

Published by
Dorchester Publishing Co., Inc.
276 Fifth Avenue
New York, NY 10001

ISBN 0-8439-4609-1

The name "Leisure Books" and its logo are trademarks of
Dorchester Publishing Co., Inc.

Printed in the United States of America.

CONTENTS

THE RIDER
OF DISTANT TRAILS

I

Buck Duane stood silently in the entrance of the Osage Saloon, his hands parting the batwings. Behind him, the late morning sun climbed slowly out of the jagged foothills and threw his shadow into the saloon.

The shadow did not reveal the man. His apparel was the ordinary outfit of the cowboy, without vanity, and it was torn and travel-stained. His boots showed evidence of an intimate acquaintance with cactus. He was a giant in stature, well over six feet of hard bone and muscle. Another striking thing about him was his somber face with its piercing eyes, and hair white over the temples.

He packed two guns, both low down—but that was too common a thing to attrack notice. The flaring butt of an ivory-handled Colt .45 which had belonged to his father was in a polished holster that was tied to his right leg. Another .45, a twin of his father's gun, was holstered on his left side.

Duane took in the interior of the saloon, noted the men at the bar, and the four men at a table at the end of the bar. A den of thieves, he thought. He had been persuaded by Captain MacNelly to return to the Texas Rangers, on secret Ranger service, to run down, capture or kill the bandit gang warring against banks, mail cars, and stage-coaches throughout Texas.

Captain MacNelly, who had obtained a pardon for Buckley Duane from the Governor of Texas after Duane's three years as an outlaw, was a slightly built man with a black mustache and hair, sharp black eyes, regular features, a peace officer who was dedicated to the law and determined to rid Texas of rustlers, bandits, and killers.

"Buck," MacNelly said, "I did you a good turn when you needed one. You served me well, that I allow. I can't forget that you rid Texas of Cheseldine and his gang. You were the only man who could have done that. I need you again. This gang is even tougher than Cheseldine's was. I need the fastest gun in Texas and you're it."

"You're making it awfully hard for me to refuse, Captain. I owe you a lot, I know, but I was thinking of setting up a little spread, finding me a wife and settling down. But—"

"Buck, you do this for me and I'll see that you get your little spread. The Governor is a friend of mine. He'll deed you some land, a good piece of property on which you can really build your spread. Well, Buck?"

"What's the deal on this mission?"

"Well, my information is that a so-called solid citizen, a man with a big spread just north of Rio Grande, is the brains of this gang. He's behind all the bank robberies, the mail car and stage-coach robberies. The leader of these bandits is a man named Tulsa Harrow, a gun-slinger with a rep of having killed twenty men. He's fast. That we know.

"But I *know* you're faster. I've seen the likes of Billy the Kid, Wyatt Earp, and Johnny Ringo. They were fast too. But you've got something they never had. Speed and calculation. You play to the other man's weakness, that delicate, split-second timing the other man uses up and you use to advantage.

"You can break up this kind of gang by taking their leader. You take him and we'll take the gang. But most important, I want the man behind the gang. That's the rancher. His name's Jonathan Finley. That much we know. I'm asking you as a friend for this favor. Come back to Company A. The Rangers need you."

Duane thought a long time before he answered. There was his mother, sister, and Uncle Jim. They needed him too. They were dependent upon him. He said as much to Captain MacNelly.

"I know," MacNelly answered. "I'll see to it they are well cared for. What's your answer now?"

Duane stuck out his hand and MacNelly shook it, a broad smile breaking the corners of his mouth and lighting up his face.

"Write me, or wire me if you can, care of the adjutant at Austin, just as you did before. But be careful. Don't risk your safety or your life."

So Buckley Duane set out on his mission of death. His horse, Bullet, seemed delighted to be out in open country again. The animal was a magnificent specimen, coal black, big, strong, and fast, and his endurance over grueling hours of riding was astonishing. Bullet carried a huge black, silver-ornamented saddle of Mexican make, a lariat and canteen, and a small pack rolled into a tarpauline.

There was a strange rapport between man and beast that held within the character of its existence a wonderful mystique most men would find puzzling. The animal seemed to know, by its own sixth sense, just where and how his master wanted him to go.

Buck Duane treated the horse with the greatest of kindness and understanding. A low whistle would bring the black to him at a gallop, its beautiful head shaking up and down, its eyes alert, standing with restrained but eager impatience to be mounted and to run with the wind.

Duane had ridden slowly as often as he had with the great speed of the black, resting himself and the horse. He slept in the quiet of the night that was lighted softly by a silver moon and soothed by the murmuring sounds of a caressing wind and a flowing stream.

Buck Duane came at last to the crest of a hill that overlooked the town of Tafton and was absorbed in a view of the country. The country wasn't as rugged as some bits he had seen. Its hills were lower, its valleys were shallower, its gorges not so wild, its mountains not so gigantic.

He visioned something here that he had not been able to

11

see in other parts of the country—the evidence of a man's efforts to turn a waste of world into a garden spot. He wondered why and for whom.

The Ranger dismounted and let Bullet graze while he searched far up the gorge behind the town, saw the frowning wall of a great dam blocking the gorge, the glint of the sun on the spraying water of the spillways. He looked over Tafton into the vast level country beyond it where man had left his mark on the soil. Herculean, persistent effort, stubborn patient, heroic sacrifice, had been contributed to the accomplishment.

Beyond, at a distance of perhaps three or four miles, the rimming hills, silent, immutable, seemed to watch indifferently. It was a wild section, wooded, with stretches of dense undergrowth. Tall sacaton grass grew here; there were great stretches of it. Farther south were low, rounded hills and timber. He marked the section in his mind. It would be a good place in which to take refuge if it ever became necessary.

As he stood there looking down at the valley and the big white house which he had already decided belonged to Jonathan Finley, he heard the sharp crack of a breaking twig below him. He stood rigid, listening, and saw a man come into view around the shoulder of the ridge, on the ledge.

The man was tall, slender, old. He wore a faded woollen shirt, trousers that were stuck into the creased and wrinkled tops of well-worn high-heeled boots that were adorned with spurs. A cartridge belt encircled his waist, supporting a holster in which was a heavy six-shooter. A battered wide-brimmed hat was in his left hand, while balanced in his right hand was a rifle.

He was directly below Buck Duane. Looking down, Duane could see the crown of his head, a bald spot where the sparse gray hair had fallen out.

There was a sinister stealthiness in the man's manner. He moved along the ledge until he was behind some dense brush. Then he dropped his hat on the ledge, and sank to his knees behind the screen of the brush at the edge. He stuck the muzzle of the rifle through the brush and waited.

Several times during the next few minutes Duane heard the man muttering to himself. He could not catch the words, but from the voice he gathered that the man was beset with a terrible impatience. Twice he raised the rifle and glanced along the sights, only to lower the weapon and curse audibly.

Although Duane could still catch glimpses of the tall man walking about the yard that surrounded the white ranch-house, he was reluctant to believe that the man kneeling below him meant to kill him. But if the tall man was Jonathan Finley, then perhaps he had good reason.

Duane waited, watching, his muscles tensed, for the kneeling man's intentions to become plain. When he saw the rifle come up again, and observed that the muzzle seemed to be following the movements of the tall figure in the yard, he leaped outward and downward. He did not want Jonathan Finley dead yet.

He landed on the ledge beside the man, lunged against him, and grasped the rifle as it exploded. As he bowled the man over upon his back and sat astride him, he had a mental picture of the white smokestreak from the rifle belching downward into the gully. Therefore, he knew that the bullet had not found its mark.

He said nothing, but his movements were swift, sure, and vigorous. He wrenched the rifle from the astonished would-be murderer and hurled it into the gully. Then he jerked the heavy six-shooter from the holster at the man's waist and threw it after the rifle. Then he settled his weight heavily upon the man's stomach and pinned his arms to the floor of the rock ledge in spread-eagle fashion. A cold wrath blazed in the man's eyes.

"Why did you want to kill him?" Duane said. "Who is he?"

"Jonathan Finley, that's who he is. A gol-danged murderer. He ain't no good. He's choked all us homesteaders, taken the good bits of land and left us dirt nothin' will grow in. Now leave me be. You've done what you were sent for, but how you knew I'll never be able to reckon."

He struggled under Duane, although he knew that his strength was not equal to that of the man who had thwarted him, and he lay back breathing hard, his eyes glaring with hatred.

"You're one of 'em ain't you?" he gasped. "One of Finley's guns. I ain't seen you before, so who be you?"

"I'm not one of Finley's men. That ought to be enough. I just don't want you killing him. You would have been in bad trouble for sure." Duane got up, yanked the old man to his feet. "You had better get out of here before Finley wakes up to the fact that you were trying to kill him."

"That I didn't is thanks to you, and you'll be regrettin' it, mister, whether you be one of Finley's men or not."

"That's strange talk at a time like this. I could be one of Finley's men and just throw you over this hill into the gully and no one would be the wiser. Get back to your home and forget about this. You'll be better off."

The old man uttered a low curse and half-stumbled as he ran from the scene. Duane brushed the dirt and dust from his clothes and stared down toward the west where there were grouped the rough houses of homesteaders set in level country through which ran the dark gashes of irrigation ditches. The level was dotted with the shacks, tent-houses and outbuildings of the homesteaders, and scratched with new roads and trails. Here and there went thin lines of fence, between which were small emerald stretches of growing crops.

II

Buck Duane heard a sudden rasping and crackling behind him, then a light step on the rock floor of the ledge; heard the rustle of garments. Then, when he still did not turn, a voice, calm, even slightly challenging, came close behind him.

"Stranger, I expect you saved Uncle Jonathan's life."

Her voice was distinctly and mellowly Southern. But in it seemed to be a note of mockery, elusive, gentle. She was tall, although her head did not quite reach his shoulder.

14

She was slender, graceful. She stood with her hands hanging with unconscious ease at her sides as if she took no thought of them whatever. Nor were they brown and rough as he had expected they would be after hearing her. Instead, they were slender, shapely, and white.

She held her slim young body erect with a dignity that rather astonished Duane although he could not understand why he had gained the impression that he would find her undignified. That she had concealed herself behind the bushes may have furnished the foundation for the impression.

"I didn't know who he was, and I didn't know he was your uncle. I just didn't care to see him killed."

"Why?" There was a curiosity in her tone and in the way she accented the word.

The Ranger thought her eyes held a vague twinkle in them. They were deep blue eyes, clear as pools of sparkling water, steady, and confident. He saw a rifle balanced against a sapling at her right hand, then looked back to her and noted that her hair gleamed like burnished gold in the sun that was streaming down upon her. It was coiled about her head in heavy, bulging waves.

"I just said why. I didn't care to see him killed."

"You go about caring about not seeing anyone killed? Is that your business?"

"Nope. But if I see someone trying to kill a man I wouldn't feel right unless I tried to stop it. Your uncle was defenseless. It was like shooting a pig in a pen."

"My uncle wouldn't like that."

"I didn't mean to imply he was a pig. I was just trying to draw a comparison."

"Between my uncle and a pig?" Her mouth turned upwards into a thin smile. She was obviously enjoying Duane's discomfort, the manner in which he kept getting deeper and deeper into a flustered condition.

He said on a note of mild defiance, "Your uncle isn't a pig!"

"Mister," she said, "lest you think of yourself as a hero, I want to tell you that I had a bead on him. I saw you too. I saw you watching him, and then when you leaped on

15

him I waited to see what would happen. So, you see, you just beat me to him. Matter of fact, you didn't save my uncle's life, you save that old coot's life. Understand?"

He smiled at her. "Just as you say, Miss—"

"Miss? Yes. Miss Catherine Finley. My father was Jonathan Finley's brother. He was killed in the War Between the States when I was still a child. Were you in the war?"

"Nope."

"If you had been, would you have been a Blue or a Gray?" Her eyes looked directly into his and she obviously wanted an answer.

He smiled showing even white teeth. "A Gray. I was born in Texas. Both my parents were Southerners. Does that please you?"

"I'm not sure. What's your name?"

"Duane. Buckley Duane. My friends call me Buck.

"Buck. All right, Buck. My friends call me Cathy. You can call me Cathy too. But that's as far as you can go. My uncle doesn't cotton to strangers. What are you doing in this neck of the woods?"

"Looking for a job."

"There aren't any. There's nothing but trouble in Tafton. I'd advise you to move on."

Duane's senses had grasped her first as a complete picture. In his astonishment of the beauty of it he did not attempt to fix details in his mind. Now he observed the white, rounded firmness of her chin and throat, and his gaze rested momentarily on her lips, which were what a woman's lips ought to be. Without warning he took her in his arms, held her tightly, and kissed her.

She didn't struggle and she didn't respond. When he let her go, she asked, "Why did you do that?" There was no anger in her voice, merely curiosity.

"You looked too beautiful to resist, that's all." He smiled broadly. "If you intend to kill me, go ahead. It was worth it."

"I just may do that." She paused. "Did you just want this one kiss or are you interested in me?"

"I'm interested."

"Why?"

Her manner of asking one-word questions was a little upsetting to Duane. He thought that perhaps it was her youth, her candidness, ingenuousness, for she could not be more than eighteen or nineteen.

"Well, that's hard to say," he said. "I think that perhaps it's—well, because you're natural."

"What do you mean?" She was looking straight at him, her clear eyes unshadowed by any sign of duplicity or guile. But for all that he felt she was probing him, seeking indications of insincerity, of equivocation, of levity. "Why shouldn't I be natural? Do you mean there are people who aren't?"

"I'm pretty certain I mean that," he told her. "There are folks who aren't."

"I don't think I'd care to know them," she declared, her eyes appearing to snap scornfully, and her wonderfully firm chin tilting upward a little. "Why should anyone pretend to be what they aren't? Can't people see they are pretending? You're not pretending, are you?" Her eyes gazed at him with an unwavering steadiness.

"Of course not."

"Do you like people who do pretend?"

"I keep as far away from them as possible."

"And yet you know people who are natural?"

"Quite a few."

"Then why do you say you are interested in me? Why are you not interested in other people who are natural?"

"I am, of course."

He thought he saw a shade of disappointment in her eyes, and he observed that the toe of one of her shoes was digging into a small hummock of earth with a movement that was almost vindictive.

"I suppose those natural folks are girls," she said, not looking at him.

He wanted to disclaim that. He did, and he could not repress a smile over the astonishing thought that she resented his admitting interest in other girls.

She had been watching him covertly; she saw the smile and her cheeks flamed, paled. She stood erect and looked at him disdainfully.

"Mr. Buck Duane," she said coldly, "I think you are pretending. You are pretending, aren't you?"

"No, I'm not."

"I see. Would you like to kiss me again?" she asked.

"Yes, I would. Very much."

"Then why don't you?"

He started to take her in his arms; but before he could, her hand lashed out and she slapped him across the face. She turned then and walked westward on the ledge. She held her head very high, and her little body was defiantly straight.

Duane stood watching her until she disappeared behind a jutting shoulder of the ridge. Then he smiled again, this time thinly, although with a strange feeling of satisfaction that she had so unmistakably betrayed jealousy. Amazed, and unaware of his own feelings, he did nonetheless experience an exhilaration he had never before known. He stood staring at the ledge where she had disappeared.

Suddenly, a rifle crashed. He felt his hat rise and settle down again. He knew that a bullet had gone through the crown, for he had had that experience before. Disdaining to run or even to turn his head, he stood rigid, defiantly facing a clump of brush from which the shot had appeared to come.

The bushes parted and Cathy Finley's face appeared. She stepped into view, rifle in hand. For an instant she stood, looking at Duane. Her eyes were flashing; her cheeks were strained a bright crimson. But despite her evident scorn and anger there was the merest shadow of a reluctant smile on her lips.

"Mr. Buck Duane," she said, "you've got nerve. Why didn't you run?"

"Cathy," he said, and bowed low, "I never run from anyone who interests me." He straightened up and saw that she was smiling.

"I'll remember that," she threw back, and then, obviously on impulse, blew him a kiss and was gone.

He whistled low and Bullet came trotting over, his head bobbing up and down in eagerness to be off again. Duane mounted and rode slowly towards town. He saw that Jonathan Finley's land made a cosmic sweep upward toward a distant mountain range. Through the slumberous haze of the morning he saw the green of gigantic stretches of grazing land; the knobs of hills with their films of pine, their bases linked with purple shadows.

The sun, now swimming high, was streaming down into a clearing that surrounded the ranch-house. He could see the white gravel walks curving around the grounds and the tall man whom he now knew to be Jonathan Finley walking about aimlessly, a cigar in his mouth.

He saw the big white house, a two-story affair with a peaked roof and three chimneys which rose majestically toward the blue sky. The house, grounds, and the man who walked about seemed to hold a strange fascination for him. It also troubled him because of Cathy.

III

Duane came into town at a leisurely gait, was struck by the atmosphere of quiet calm which pervaded it. There was a vacuum-like silence. The Osage Saloon was a combination saloon and hotel. It was a rambling frame building with a wide porch running across its front with a sign hanging under the eaves bearing the legend: OSAGE SALOON AND HOTEL.

Across the dirt road was a row of other frame buildings, low and squat which housed a general store, a barber shop, restaurant, blacksmith shop, express office, and several other buildings that were occupied by merchants. He dismounted and tied Bullet to the hitch-rail, walked up the two low steps to the batwings, opened them and stood there for a long moment.

As Duane stood there he saw four pairs of hostile eyes turned on him from a table at the farthest corner of the saloon to the left of the long bar which ran from the entrance to the end of the room. Half a dozen men stood at

19

the bar drinking and talking but these paid no attention to him. He walked in slowly, with a measured step, and the four pairs of eyes followed him each step of the way as he moved to the center of the bar.

"Whiskey," he told the bartender. As a bottle of whiskey and a glass were set on the bar before him. Duane sensed that the bartender, a man of medium height, slim but wiry, agile in his movements, and carrying a six-gun strapped to his left leg in a short holster, was somehow connected with the gang.

The Ranger wondered if the mark of the lawman showed so much in his face and appearance that the bartender recognized it, or if, possibly, the fact that he was a stranger in town was responsible for the interest in him. As he poured himself a drink, one of the men at the table stood up and walked to the bar, stopped a few feet from where Buck Duane stood.

The man was Slap Wilson, a gunfighter. Duane took him in with a quick glance, saw how Wilson's holster was tied to his right leg, at the right distance to permit a swift and easy draw. He saw, too, that the leather of the holster was greased slick and bright to allow the .44 Colt an un-hampered draw.

"You riding through, stranger?" Wilson asked.

"Don't know. Been riding a long time. Thought I'd look about a bit."

"Ain't nothin' to look about in this town," Wilson answered. "It's a nice, quiet little town. Ain't much doin' hereabouts."

"So I noticed. Must be nigh onto eight o'clock. Don't nobody work around here?"

"Yep. But not before eight thirty. Half an hour from now all the stores will be open and people will be comin' into town."

So late?

"Kind of queer, ain't it?"

"Not so queer. There's goin' to be a trial today. Fella by the name of Tulsa Harrow's goin' to be on trial."

The name struck a bell in Duane's mind. Tulsa Harrow. The man Captain MacNelly had said was the leader of the gang. "What's he done?" he asked.

"Ain't done nothin'. Some crazy homesteader says he burned his shack and killed two of his cows. Ever hear of Tulsa Harrow?"

"Nope. Can't say I have."

"Where you from, stranger?"

"Galveston."

"That's a long way from here. How come?"

"You really want to know?"

"That's why I'm askin'."

"Well, kind of had to leave quick like, if you know what I mean."

Wilson eyed him narrowly. "What kind of job you lookin' for?"

"Don't matter. I'm good at a lot of things."

Wilson pointed to the guns strapped to Duane's legs, "I see. Includin' those."

Duane hesitated a moment then said, "Including those."

Wilson flipped a silver dollar from a pocket in his shirt, held it between a thumb and forefinger and suddenly threw it into the air and yelled, "*Draw!*"

Duane's movement was so fast that Wilson's word had barely died down when the shot exploded, and the silver dollar tumbled crazily in the air and then fell to the floor, creased dead center. Every pair of eyes stared at him with fascinated wonder.

Slap Wilson said, "I think you'll do. I think Tulsa Harrow will be inclined to hire you." He hesitated a moment then said, "He's that fast too. Maybe faster."

"Tulsa Harrow? But you said he was going on trial today."

Wilson laughed. "That I did, but I didn't say he would be convicted. He won't be." He turned to the bartender. "Sal, give this gent a drink. That kind of shootin' calls for a drink. Come on, boys, belly up to the bar. Drinks on me."

"No," Duane answered. "On me. I did the shooting."

"You didn't give me your handle, stranger. If you're buyin' the drinks we ought to know who you are."

21

The Ranger looked around the room as the men came to the bar from the table at the far end. "Buck Duane, boys."

"This here's Buck Duane, Sal. Hear? Looks like he might be with us. Set it up!"

Wilson introduced him to each man at the bar. "Stu. Harry. Bob. Frank." The first three were the ones who had sat at the table with him. Frank, obviously, was the leader of the group that had been standing at the bar when he came in. All the men were dressed in blue jeans, boots, wool shirts, kerchiefs around their legs, and guns tied low on their legs.

Gun-fighters all—one faster than the other, Duane thought. None of them mattered, he told himself. None, that is, except Slap Wilson. He recognized him instantly from the description of Captain MacNelly had given him of the gang. So there would be two Duane had to watch, and perhaps fight in a gun duel. Slap Wilson and Tulsa Harrow.

About a half hour later Slap Wilson said, "Well, boys, I think it's 'bout time we went to the courthouse to watch that there trial. Let's go." He turned to Duane. "Come along, Buck. I think you'll find this kind of interestin'."

The courthouse was in a frame building a block away from the Osage Saloon and Hotel. As the men emerged from the saloon, Buck Duane saw that the street was no longer vacant or quiet. Benches were occupied by visitors who evidently had reached Tafton while he had been in the saloon. Women in calico gowns dotted the place with color; children were racing over the grass and the walks; men walked about or stood in groups talking.

Around the edge of the square where the courthouse was situated were wagons, buckboards, buggies. Ponies bearing saddles were hitched to various racks. The space in front of the courthouse was thick with vehicles of various descriptions.

Duane stopped to buy a hat in a store near the courthouse. He crumpled the other and threw it into an empty barrel that stood near the entrance. Duane turned and addressed the storekeepr.

22

"Expecting any trouble today?"

The storekeeper looked Duane over quickly. "I hope not. This Tulsa Harrow—well, I don't know. Better not say anything. If you go to the courthouse you'll understand. Judge Grant lives right here in Tafton. Didn't want to handle the case but couldn't get anyone else to sit in."

"I see. Well, I think I'll just go over to the courthouse and have a look at the proceedings."

Duane crossed the square and entered the courthouse. The large square room was already filled to capacity but Duane found a space in a corner and stood there, his eyes taking in the men who stood around him and Judge Grant, who sat behind a desk at the back of the room. Inside the railing which separated the spectators from the court officials and the defendant he saw Cathy. Seated next to her was a tall, distinguished looking man who could be Jonathan Finley.

At a table a few feet from where Cathy and Finley sat was another tall man, obviously the defendant, Tulsa Harrow. On the opposite side of the table was a small, slim man in a loose fitting dark suit who, very likely was the prosecutor. Duane's eyes were fixed on Tulsa Harrow.

He saw that Tulsa Harrow was young, no more than thirty, broad of shoulder, slim of waist, with long arms and strong hands with long tapering fingers. Duane felt he could beat this man in a fight. He had been told Harrow was fast, maybe even faster than he was. If that were so, then the thing that was in his favor would be in the split-second error in movement, the timelessness when the draw for the gun would be made. He dismissed the probability of his own error as Cathy turned, saw him, gave him a quick smile and turned her head.

A voice beside him broke up his thoughts of Cathy. "Watch the show, Duane. This'll be good." It was Slap Wilson.

Duane nodded.

The prosecutor was looking over some papers. His face was in profile to Duane, so he couldn't tell much about him. Judge Grant rapped his gavel on the desk and nodded to the bailiff, who held up his hands for silence and then announced that Court was open and in session.

"Mr. Meadows," Judge Grant said, "you may proceed."

The prosecutor arose from his seat, looked about nervously, then said, "Your Honor, we are concerned in this trial with the defendent, Mr. Tulsa Harrow, who is charged with burning down the home of the plaintiff, Mr. Clem Abbott. I call Mr. Abbott to the stand."

The plaintiff called out in a loud voice, "Mr. Abbott is here. I am ready to testify." He turned and pointed a finger at Tulsa Harrow. "He burned down my house and killed two of my three milk cows."

There was a loud murmuring of voice among the spectators and Judge Grant rapped his gavel for silence. "Mr. Abbott, you will have to take the stand and testify from there. Take the stand and be sworn in."

The plaintiff, a slight man in his fifties, bent, his hands showing years of work with hoe and rake, was dressed in a pair of bib-overalls, a brown wool shirt, and dirty, worn boots. He strode to the stand, was sworn in, and sat down. He seemed to be staring at Tulsa Harrow for several seconds and then turned his eyes.

Buck Duane saw that Tulsa Harrow was looking straight into the face of the witness, his gaze fixed intently on Clem Abbott, who began shifting around nervously in his seat. There were many more homesteaders in the audience than Harrow men, or Duane thought, Jonathan Finley men. The homesteaders obviously were looking toward Abbott to make a break in the hold Finley and Harrow had on the town. If a conviction could be gotten, and it all depended on Abbott's testimony, on his courage to face down the gang, then there was some hope for them.

Duane looked around at the various members of the gang—Slap Wilson, Stu, Bob, Harry, Frank and the others. Some were smiling, others had sneers on their faces as they looked toward the witness stand. He felt sorry for the homesteaders.

These people who were striving for fairness in the law, for an opportunity to build lives for themselves in this outlaw-infested community, to progress in a civilization that was still raw and untamed, were defeated and thwarted by that faith in the law and the court which administered its justice. That was obvious to him. Judge Grant was a weakling. The prosecutor was no better.

The homesteaders would not fight with guns, and if they did they would die doing it because they were no match for this gang of thugs, all of whom were gunfighters, one better than the other. Still, they were there to voice their protests, to demand that a guilty man be punished for his crimes, that the sovereignty of the law be upheld.

How many times they had been defeated in this courtroom Buck Duane didn't know, but he was certain it was more than once. The law that operated in Tafton was not a constitutional law but a Jonathan Finley law. That, too, was obvious to Duane.

The prosecutor asked Clem Abbott to describe the events of May second. "What happened on that day and what did you see?"

"Well, it was nigh onto dusk and me and my wife Bessie was in the field working when I looked up and saw my house burning, and then this man rode up to where my milch cows were grazing and he shot one of them, and I hollered at him, and then he shot the other cow, and I started to run to where he was but afore I got there he rode off."

The prosecutor said, "You stated in your testimony that you saw 'this man.' Who did you mean? Is that man in this court now? Do you see him here?"

Clem Abbott rose from his chair and pointed a finger at Tulsa Harrow. "That's him right there! He did it!"

IV

There was a loud murmur of voices again, most of the sounds coming from the homesteaders who, no doubt, were certain this positive identification would result in a conviction. Judge Grant would have no alternative but to hand down a guilty verdict.

The prosecutor turned in several directions, uneasy, nervous, not knowing how next to proceed. He very likely had hoped for a vauge identification that would take him off the hook, because he didn't want to convict Tulsa Harrow. That was as plain to Buck Duane as the brightness of the day. The proesecutor looked toward Judge Grant, shrugged his shoulders.

At this point, Jonathan Finley stood up. Duane fixed his eyes on him, saw him full face and in profile. Finley was tall, straight as a ramrod, with hair as white as seeding clematis and gleaming like snow on a mountain peak with the sun shining upon it. It was rich and abundant, with a virility that made it stand out upon his head with a hint of waviness, suggesting the ghosts of curls that had been there in his younger days.

Finley was as erect as a well-trained military officer standing at attention. But he was infinitely more at ease because he was apparently unconscious of himself, was giving no thought to himself. He stood there for a long minute and stared at Clem Abbott, his keen blue eyes flecked with tiny points of fire, of challenging inquiry. It was as if this white-haired man mutely demanded to know why this miserable wretch, this poor tenant farmer, a homesteader without a piece of land of his own, could voice an accusation that was so groundless.

Duane studied him intently, saw that the man's features were large, bold, his skin a raw bronze. Perhaps the face had once been handsome, for there were still signs of an intensely masculine comeliness in the lines of nose and mouth and chin; but character, developing, had set its stamp upon his countenance. That character was similar to the shark or the barracuda. The man was arrogant, inflexible, a persuader of robbery and murder, a man surely with no conscience, no compassion.

Duane marked him as a dangerous man, more so even than Tulsa. He could understand, however, from whose side of the family Cathy had inherited her looks. The blue eyes, chin, nose, and mouth were Finley, more finely formed, true, more delicate, but the lines were all there. He wondered if she had also inherited some of his nature, and as he wondered about it he told himself that he hoped she hadn't.

Jonathan Finley looked toward Judge Grant, pointed a finger at the ceiling as he spoke. "Judge, any evidence that's been given here ain't worth a damn!"

The homesteaders began to murmur again, some in loud voices, as they saw their hopes for a conviction in the case dwindle and fade with each word Jonathan Finley uttered.

"I've known Tulsa Harrow for ten years. I've never known him to do a mean or low thing in all that time."

The Ranger saw the broad smiles on the faces of the gang. They were smiles of amusement. The faces of the homesteaders were grim.

"This here homesteader, this man, Clem Abbott, comes into this court and says he saw Tulsa Harrow. He said it was dusk. He said he was in the field. I know his place. The field is a good hundred yards, that's three hundred feet, from his shack, and from where his cows were grazing. How the hell is he going to recognize anybody from that distance?"

Judge Grant nodded his head.

Jonathan Finley turned his attention to Clem Abbott. "You wear glasses, don't you?" he asked in a towering voice.

Abbott stood up from his chair and stared mutely at Finley.

"I asked you if you wear glasses!" Finley repeated.

"Yes I do. But I can see without them too," he answered defiantly.

"Sure you can," Finley declared. "You can see your two feet and hands, and that's about all. For all you know, some wild kid could've rode up and burned your shack as a prank, and then shot your cows. Isn't that right?"

Abbott didn't answer, just stood there and looked back at his tormentor with tired and defeated eyes. There was dead silence in the room. Duane saw the homesteaders bow their heads, their backs bend, their shoulders droop. The whole scene stabbed at him with a mixture of sadness and anger.

27

Judge Grant was visibly disturbed. He reddened, fumbled with the papers that lay before him on the desk. He finally spoke. "I'm inclined to believe the defendant is innocent, since there has been no positive proof presented here that he was the man who committed the offense charged."

Abbott's eyes filled with tears. His wife, who stood near the rail which separated the spectators from the court officials wiped at her eyes with a handkerchief. So did several other women.

Jonathan Finley spoke coldly. "This seems to end this case, Judge. Abbott has proved nothing. His eyesight ain't what it used to be. He was very clearly mistaken. I'll allow that maybe his intentions were honest, but it's just as dishonest to make an accusation unfounded on fact as it is to tell a downright lie, a lie that could send a man to prison or hang him. I hope Tulsa Harrow will forgive this man who tried to do him evil."

Duane felt his stomach turn over. He had seen some raw things in his life so far but this one took the cake and all the crumbs.

Jonathan Finley walked over to Tulsa Harrow and touched him on the shoulder. "Come on, Tulsa. Get out of that chair, and let's get out of here."

Tulsa rose, brushed an imaginary fleck of dust from his coat, looked around the courtroom. He was a fox, a cheetah, a grim hunter of his fellowman, a ravager, despoiler, and a murderer. This was his native habitat and in it he was indisputably master.

Cathy stood up and joined her uncle and Tulsa, and the three started out from the courtroom. As they came to Buck Duane, Cathy said, "I'll wait for you outside."

Duane nodded his head.

When they had passed, Slap Wilson came over to Buck Duane. He was smiling broadly. "Well, how did you like the show? That Mr. Finley is really something, ain't he? Took right over. Better than any lawyer man. Come on, Buck, I'll stand for the drinks."

"Have to talk to someone first. You go ahead and I'll join you in a little while."

28

"Sure. I want you to meet Tulsa Harrow."

"I want to do that," Duane answered in a strange tone but Slap Wilson missed the significance of its meaning.

Duane moved out with the rest of the homsesteaders who were talking intently among themselves. Their faces showed plainly the great disappointment they felt. He went down the short three steps to the wooden walk and saw Cathy standing with her uncle. He went over, removed his hat.

"Uncle Jonathan," she said, "I want you to meet Mr. Buckley Duane. His friends call him Buck. He's the man who saved your life this morning."

"Thanks very much, Mr. Duane," Finley said, and held out his hand. "What made you do it?"

"I don't like to see a man shot in the back," Duane answered pointedly. "That's what he was fixin' to do to you."

"I see," Finley said thoughtfully. Then, "My niece tells me you're looking for a job. That right?"

"Yes, sir."

"Cowhand?"

"I can do that too."

"Meaning you prefer something else?"

"If it's available."

"Well, let me think about it. Come see me tomorrow afternoon and I may have an answer for you."

While they were talking, buggies, spring-wagons, buckboards, and other vehicles were wheeling away amid dust that swirled in clouds. Horses bearing riders were cavorting around the square, then heading for open country. The square had been magically cleared, with the exception of about a dozen people who were walking toward the various stores on the street. A man approached Finley from the south, stopped before him.

"Mr. Finley," the man said, "my name's Kelly. Jeff Kelly. I own a piece of land 'bout three miles south of town."

"What can I do for you, Mr. Kelly?"

Kelly was a short, stocky man with a full mustache. He wore the blue jeans and boots of the rancher, the typical horseman. He appeared to be in his mid-thirties, strong as a blacksmith.

"I was in the courtroom this morning. I heard everything. I have something to say to you."

"Say it," Finley replied. His tone was challenging.

"Mr. Finley, there ain't so much law in this country but what a man's got some right in the place where he lives. You bluffed that judge and you bluffed the prosecutor. I don't know what kind of hold you got on 'em but what you did in there this morning was to destroy every law on the books and every right a man has to live under it peacefully.

"If your man Harrow didn't burn down that farmer's shack and shoot his cows then there ain't a steer in Texas. That's what I think."

Finley's face paled with anger for a fleeting second and his eyes glittered with rage, but he took hold of himself quickly. "Mr. Kelly, I hold to the idea that every man has a right to his opinion. That's yours."

Cathy's blue eyes narrowed and remained so as she spoke. "Mr. Kelly, I think you're a damned fool! You're accusing my uncle of running the court. What he did was to defend an innocent man. That right was his!"

"I've got no quarrel with you, Miss. I wouldn't think of it. But like your uncle said, everybody has a right to his opinion."

As they stood there talking, Tulsa Harrow strolled over from across the street. He was wearing his gun, a Colt .44 with a silver handle. "Howdy, folks. Something I should listen to?"

"Yes, you should," Cathy said. "This is Mr. Kelly. He's accusing Uncle Jonathan of having bluffed the judge and prosecutor into freeing you this morning."

Tulsa looked down at Kelly. He was at least six inches taller than the man he faced. "Mr. Kelly, eh? I know who you are. You got a spread south of town. Nice place. You also got a wife and two kids, a boy and a girl. Right?"

Tulsa's tone was even, smooth, as if he were discussing the weather. His voice didn't change as he said, "Mr. Kelly, Mr. Finley is a friend of mine. I don't like anybody

30

talking dirt to my friends. The next time you do it you'll die so fast you'll think somebody is shovin' you. Understand?"

"Yes, I understand," Kelly replied, but there was no fear in his tone. "I don't wear a gun. I'm not a gunfighter. I was brought up to respect the law and to live under it whether it be a good law or a bad law. Every homesteader in this territory has been pushed farther and farther back from the land Mr. Finley wanted. I reckon he wants the land Abbott is working. I reckon you'll get it for him."

"Your mouth is goin' to dig you a quick grave, Mr. Kelly," Tulsa said softly. "Take my advice and put a button on it. That's all. Understand? *That's all*." The last two words were said in an unmistakably menacing tone.

Duane noticed a peculiar thing at that moment. When Tulsa spoke those two words his left foot moved just a fraction to the left and his right shoulder drooped. He marked it down in his mind.

Jeff Kelly nodded to Cathy, turned and walked toward the buckboard across the road, got in, and drove away.

"Don't worry about him none, Mr. Finley," Tulsa said. "He'll never bother you again. I'll see to that."

"I wasn't worried none, Tulsa. Oh, by the way, this young man is looking for a job. He saved my life this morning. Some damned fool tried to shoot me from atop a hill whie I was walking in the yard. This man jumped him, disarmed him, and booted him away."

Tulsa turned to Buck Duane, extended his hand. "Glad to know you. My name's Tulsa Harrow."

"I know. Slap Wilson told me about you this morning. I met him in the Osage. My name's Duane. Buck Duane."

"Were you in court this morning?" Tulsa asked.

"Yep. I was interested."

"What'd you think of it?"

"I didn't think about it," Duane lied. "The evidence didn't prove a thing. That's all I went on." That part was true. Yet if the evidence hadn't upheld the letter of the law, it had, in fact, upheld the spirit.

Tulsa Harrow looked Duane over a little closer, a quick glance from head to foot. "Handy with those pieces of iron?'' he asked, and pointed to the guns strapped to Duane's legs.

"Pretty handy."

"Mr. Finley said you wanted a job."

"I'll talk to him tomorrow, Tulsa. After you and I talk abouit it. Well, let's go, Cathy. See me after lunch, Tulsa."

"Sure thing, Mr. Finley."

Cathy Finley gave Duane a quick, secret smile, winked at him, and then she put her hand in one of her uncle's and the two walked toward home, heads high, a king and a princess of a small domain.

V

It was apparent to Buck Duane that Jonathan's one weakness was his niece. It wasn't hard to explain. She was all he had in the world other than his money, land, the stock, possibly the largest in the state of Texas, and power. Dangerous? Duane let out a low whistle.

Tulsa Harrow said, "Did you say something, Buck?"

"Nope. Just whistled. I promised Slap Wilson I'd meet him in the Osage. Care to join us?"

"Now now. I have a few things to take care of. I'll see you tomorrow."

Harrow cocked his head a little and gave Duane another once-over in that quick way he had, turned without a word and walked to his horse, mounted, and rode away.

Duane watched Tulsa until he was out of sight and thought, "So that's Tulsa Harrow. I guess I'll do a little practicing on quick draws. Yes, sir. It sure calls for it."

The Ranger walked slowly toward the Osage, his mind tumbling. Finley. Cathy. Tulsa. Wilson. It all fitted, and yet it didn't fit. There was a piece missing the puzzle, a very small piece, an important and integral piece. That could be the key to the whole thing.

In the Osage, Slap Wilson met Buck Duane with a loud

yell. "Been waitin' for you, Buck. Drink up! Sal, another bottle!"

Most of the men, and there were about fifteen in the group, were about half-drunk, celebrating Tulsa's freedom. They were noisy, laughing, telling ribald stories, slapping each other on the back and yelling for more whiskey. Duane drank moderately. Then Slap suggested a shooting contest.

"Five dollars a man. Stu, me, and you, Buck. What do you say? One time only. Winner pick up the money, and buys the drinks. You on?"

Duane shrugged. "What've I got to lose? How we going to settle it?"

"Give us three empty bottles, Sal. We'll take these outside and set 'em up on a fence, alongside the barber shop. There's about twenty feet of field there. Just right. First one to break the bottle wins. One shot only."

"Who'll call?" Duane asked.

"Harry. He's good at callin'. Once called me in a poker game when I had an ace full." He laughed and everyone laughed with him except Harry.

"I thought he was bluffin'."

"That's the big trick, Harry," Wilson said. "To know when a man's bluffin' an' when he's tryin' to run a whizzer. Let's go, boys!"

The group filed out, ran to the side of the barber shop where Harry set up the bottles about ten feet apart. The three men took positions in the field some twenty feet from where the bottles stood on the fence.

Slap and Stu adjusted their holsters, moved their guns up and down to test their slide. Duanne watched each man as he did this but could note nothing that would reveal a possible flaw in their draws.

"Ready?" Harry asked.

"Not yet!" Bob yelled. "I want to make a side bet. Ten dollars on Slap. Any takers?"

There were none, either because the men didn't want to reveal a disbelief in Wilson's prowess or because they feared to bet against him. Duane decided to lose. Not by much. A split second would be enough considering the fact

33

that both Slap and Stu had been drinking heavily.

"All right," Harry yelled, "when I yell *draw*, then you pull and shoot. Ready?"

"Ready, ready!" Slap yelled back.

Harry waited several moments then yelled, "*Draw!*"

The three guns exploded simultaneously and all three bottles shattered.

"A tie!" Harry yelled.

It wasn't exactly true. Duane's bottle exploded a fraction of a second before the other two, and this despite the fact that he held back on his draw. It didn't mean anything, he told himself. Both men were drunk. But both were unmistakably fast. How much faster they were when they were sober was something he'd have to contemplate, to watch, and to note.

And again, there would have to be the split-second of time that would be his advantage. This, he told himself, was not going to be any pie-eating contest. This was going to be life and death, requiring the steadiest of nerves, eyes, mind, and body.

The group filed back into the Osage, more noisy than before. They continued drinking for another hour, when Buck Duane said, "Boys, I hate to leave. Must find a place to stay and get some rest."

"Say, Sal," Slap yelled, "ain't you got a room for Buck?"

"Nope. All filled up, Slap. Let him try the Widow Crowe. I think she has a room to rent. It's up the street, Buck. A brown house with green shutters. Can't miss it."

"Thanks. I'll ride over there."

Buck Duane didn't. Instead he rode south. He wanted to find Jeff Kelly's spread. Three miles, he had heard Tulsa Harrow say. Should be easy to locate. The Ranger made certain no one was following him as he rode out, located the spread, rode in, found a bucket, filled it from the well and gave Bullet a long drink. As he was doing so, Jeff Kelly came out from the house.

"Can I help you stranger?"

"Yes, you can. My name's Buck Duane."

Kelly looked him over, recognized him. "Yes. You were

34

with Mr. Finley and his niece this morning. What do you want?"

"I want to talk to you confidentially. I don't want my horse to be recognized. Can I take him around the back?"

"What do you want to talk about, Mr. Duane?"

"Something that will interest you. Something you spoke about to Mr. Finley."

Duane's manner of speaking and appearance told Kelly he could be trusted. "Yes. Bring him around to the back of the house and tie him there. Come in through the back door."

Duane led Bullet to the rear of the house, tied him to a pole, went into the house. Kelly met him at the door. Mrs. Kelly, a small, attractive woman in her late twenties, was in the kitchen.

"Sara, this is Mr. Buck Duane. I think he's a friend come to help us. Let's go into the parlor, Mr. Duane."

"Would you care for a cup of coffee, Mr. Duane?" Sara Kelly asked.

"Yes, that would be fine, thank you."

Duane noted that the house, which held several rooms, was furnished tastefully and was scrupulously clean. It reminded him of his own home, the way his mother kept the house. This was the home of a man who cared about his family, an honest man, the kind necessary to a growing community, the kind that would be interested in improving things, building schools, churches, civic projects. Mrs. Kelly brought in the coffee and left.

"You came to talk things over with me, Mr. Duane. I'm ready to listen."

"Mr. Kelly, I have to trust someone around here and you appear to be the one. I took in everything you said this morning to Mr. Finley. I liked what you said and how you handled yourself with Tulsa Harrow."

"He's a mean man. Rotten to the core. A killer. He's driven out about twenty homesteaders and gobbled up their land for Finley. He wants Abbott's land, and then he's going to move south, step by step, until he comes to me."

"I figured as much." Duane leaned forward as if to

35

emphasize a point. "Mr. Kelly, I'm a Texas Ranger, assigned to Company A under Captain MacNelly. You can check me out any way you want."

Kelly's eyebrows raised. "No need to. I believe you. I'm at your service, Mr. Duane. How can I help?"

"My job is to break up this gang, any way I can. The way I figure it, I'll have to have a showdown with Slap Wilson and Tulsa Harrow, when the time comes. Mr. Finley, when I get the goods on him, will go to prison. The gang robs banks, mail cars, stagecoaches. I'm here as an undercover man, so I'm joining the gang. Only way I can get the goods on them.

"However, I'll be tipping off Captain MacNelly any time the gang is ready to stage a robbery. That's where you come in. I very likely won't have time to post a letter or send a telegram. I'm asking you to help in that way."

"Just tell me how and I'll do it."

"I think the best way would be for you to drive into town, say every other day, at exactly ten o'clock to the general store. If I have a message to send I'll find a way to slip it to you."

"That won't be necessary. Hiram Callahan is a friend of mine. Our folks came from the same town in Ireland. You give him the message and he'll get it to me, as fast as he can. However, I will go into town every other day, just to be sure. A telegram will have to be sent from the next town. That's Anderson. Ten miles south of here. I'll ride in. I've got a fast horse."

"You'll speak to Mr. Callahan?"

"Tomorrow. I'll have him come here so there won't be any danger of anyone overhearing anything. It'll be all set. Is there anything else I can do to help?"

"No, that will be enough. For the time, don't antagonize Tulsa Harrow or any of the gang. Play it meek, submissive. Like you were scared off by Tulsa. If you should run into Mr. Finley I would suggest that you apologize to him for what you said."

"God! It would turn my stomach!"

"A turned stomach, Mr. Kelly, is better than one shot full of holes. Try to do it my way."

"All right, Mr. Duane, just as you say."

Duane rose. "I think it best that you don't tell anyone other than Mr. Callahan about our conversation. Not even your wife, for her protection and everybody else's."

"Of course, Mr. Duane." Kelly held out his hand. "You don't know how much better I feel since talking with you. I've prayed for someone like you to come along and straighten things out in this town. So has every other honest person here. It's been a nightmare, I can tell you."

"I believe it. Don't worry about it. I'll take care of it."

The way Duane said it, his manner, his complete air of confidence, authority even, made Kelly smile with relief and satisfaction. He looked now at Duane as if he were a delivering angle.

As they walked back to the kitchen, Jeff Kelly said, "Sara, Mr. Duane is a real friend. Shake hands with him."

Sara Kelly wiped her hand on her apron, held out out. "We've needed one, Mr. Duane. Any time you're hungry, please stop by. I'm a good cook." She smiled apologetically.

"I'm sure you are, and I may take you up on it, sooner than you expect."

"It'll be a pleasure."

VI

The next day Buck Duane rose early. The widow Crowe, who was much younger than he had imagined her to be, and twice as attractive, offered him breakfast.

"It goes with the room, Mr. Duane."

"Thank you, Mrs. Crowe. I guess I could stand it."

"You may call me Abby, if you wish," she said and smiled. "It's short for Abigail, which I loathe."

"All right, Abby."

The Ranger sat down at the table in the neat kitchen, watched her as she puttered around the stove in efficient movements. He judged her to be about twenty-four,

37

perhaps a year or two less. It was always hard to judge a woman's age, especially a small woman. She was small. About five feet two.

The bright yellow calico dress, while it did not reveal the trim figure, did not hide it either. She was round and firm in all the right places. Her skin had the moist, luminous glow of perfect health, and her dark hair was combed in soft waves and into a knobbed chignon.

What Duane liked about her most was her candid brown eyes and her brilliant smile. She had the whitest, most even teeth he had ever seen.

She made him a platter of bacon and eggs, and fried potatoes, took hot biscuits from the stove, and set out a jar of homemade jam.

"I preserved those myself," she said, and unscrewed the jar. "You will try some, won't you?"

"Sure. Aren't you eating?"

"Oh, Lord, I ate hours ago. I rise quite early. You see, I can't afford to loll around in no bed. I pick berries in season, put them up in jars and sell them. Also, apples, cherries, pears, plums, and vegetables. You know, I'm rather famous for that around here. Besides, I have to earn my living."

"Won't you sit down, have some coffee with me?"

"Yes, I think I will." She poured herself a cup and sat down at the opposite end of the table.

They were silent for long moments, strangers trying to bridge the gap that intervened and separated them from knowledge of each other, friendship, and intimacy. She kept her head lowered, but her eyes were raised to him in shy glances.

"Abby," Duane said at last, "what happened to your husband? You're mighty young to be a widow."

"He was killed about three years ago. He was a fine young man. I sorrowed for him for a long time."

"How was he killed?"

"In a gun fight with Tulsa Harrow."

Duane was silent for several moments, the fork of food he was holding half-raised to his mouth. "Why?" he asked.

38

"I don't know." She brushed a quick tear from her eyes. "It happened in the Osage Saloon. An argument. That's what I was told. That man Harrow came around after the funeral and tried to explain, said he was sorry it happened and would like to help me. He offered me some money but I wouldn't take it. Then he tried to kiss me, said some awful things to me."

The Ranger was thoughtful for a while then said, "You're a very attractive woman, Abby. This may be harsh, but do you think Tulsa deliberately picked an argument with your husband in order to kill him and leave the way open for him?"

"With me? Yes, I've thought of it. He came around several times after his first visit but I wouldn't allow him in the house. He's a terrible man. Everyone in the territory knows about him but they can't prove a thing, or are afraid to do it."

"I see." He changed the subject. "Abby," he said with a smile, "aren't you afraid what the townspeople will say about you having a man in your home, you being so young and pretty?"

"No, Mr. Duane, I'm not concerned. You see—"

"You're unfair, Abby. You said I could call you by your first name but you won't call me by mine. Try it. It's Buck."

She gave him a bright smile. "All right, Buck. I started to say that if I bothered to care about what people say I'd have moved from here long ago. No, I live my life. That's my privilege."

"Good girl. Abby, I want to tell you something. I'm going to work for Jonathan Finley."

Her face grew darkly serious.

"No, wait. I know all about Finley, and Harrow and the gang. I'm asking you not to judge me yet because of it. I'm asking you to trust me and believe in me. I can't tell you any more now. I hope you will, that's all."

She looked into his eyes for a long time, saw something there that satisfied her. "All right, Buck. I won't ask any questions, and I'll trust you."

He reached out and took her hand in his. "Thanks. I

appreciate that.''

When he let go of her hand she put her own over her breast and held it there for several moments, her breathing increasing in tempo. "It's been a long time since a man held my hand, Buck. I—I—oh, I don't know." She gave a nervous little laugh, and rose. "I guess I better wash up the dishes. More coffee?''

"No, thanks.'' He rose from the table, stood very close to her, put an arm around her shoulder in a friendly gesture. "Don't worry about a thing, Abby. Not a thing.''

He turned from her and started out the door, looked back and saw that she was weeping softly. But he didn't know why.

Buck Duane saddled Bullet and rode up into the hills. He thought about Finley, Harrow, and Kelly. Jeff Kelly concerned him most. The West was full of his kind—pioneers steeped in the glamor of the past, of men who blazed the trails across the nation and opened up the virgin territories, built towns, railroads, developed trade, gave to the nation its blood and energy.

Kelly was needed and had to survive; and in order to guarantee that survival, men like Finley, Harrow, Wilson, and the rest of the gang had to be destroyed. It wouldn't be easy. But as he rode over the hills and verdant valleys under the brassy sky he was aware that he was giving more thought to Cathy than he was to her uncle or Harrow. She was loyal to her uncle. He had seen that. She wouldn't admire anyone who became his enemy.

Duane loped Bullet to the top of a hill, paused there, saw the winding river which tumbled down the gorge near Tafton to splash at last over the rocky edge of a red scoria butte with a funnel-like chasm cut in its end, and go swirling and broadening to the lower country. He could see the falls from where he stood, saw that the river vanished somewhere behind the cottonwoods that surrounded the big white house. In that house were Jonathan Finley and Cathy. They bothered him, in different ways.

Duane dismounted and stood there looking out at the view before him, lost in his thoughts. His sixth sense gave him a sudden warning, and he turned to see a lone rider gentling a big roan gelding toward him. The rider came to within twenty feet of where he stood, and dismounted.

Buck Duane recognized him as one of the gang, a man in his mid-twenties, clean of face, with narrow eyes and an aquiline nose. He was wearing a brace of Colts.

"I been followin' you, Duane," the man said. "You know why?"

The Ranger eyed him thoughtfully. He had a vague idea that the man knew him for what he was. If so, there would be trouble, something he didn't want at this stage of the game. However, it seemed unavoidable.

"No, I don't know why you've been following me. Why have you?"

"You ain't that much of a fool, Mister," the young man shot back. "You know damned well why I've been following you. What I should've done was tell Tulsa Harrow who you are and let him and the boys take care o' you. But I wanted that chance myself. All alone, see? Right out here in the middle of nowhere, just you and me under the big sky."

He grinned maliciously, cocksure of himself, eyeing Buck Duane intently for any untoward move.

"You're wrong whatever you think," Duane replied. "I'm a loner, rode in looking for a chance to make some money."

"Sure you did," the young man sneered, "reward money. I got a good memory, especially for faces of lawmen. I recall you good. Cheseldine. You fit, don't you?"

Buck Duane shifted his feet a little but made no move with his hands.

The young man said, "My name's Johnny Black. Mebbe that name don't ring a bell with you but I'm better known as The Gumdrop Kid." He grinned crookedly. "That recall something to you, Mister?" he asked, a boastful pride in his voice. "The Gumdrop Kid!"

Buck Duane knew his reputation. He had killed ten men, was a braggart, dangerous as a coiled rattlesnake. The Ranger decided to try to make a deal.

"Suppose I am a lawman, Johnny? Wouldn't you be better off to turn yourself in to me, help me break up the gang?"

The Gumdrop Kid gave a short laugh. "Turn myself in to *you*?" he mocked. "I don't make no deals with no stinkin' lawmen. That's what you are, a stinkin' lawman!" As he finished speaking, Black's hand flashed to his gun.

He was a split second slow. Buck Duane's gun leaped into his hand and exploded twice, the slugs striking Johnny Black in the chest. His gun flew from his hand and he toppled over on his back.

Buck Duane walked to where the Gumdrop Kid lay, looked down at him. The glassy eyes moved slightly, centered, and were still. The Ranger knew he was dead. The killing presented a problem to him. Johnny Black would be missed, and if his roan gelding came into town without its rider the gang would go looking for him. Well, he'd just have to bluff it out, play it by ear.

Duane led Bullet away from the scene, walked back and covered his tracks, reloaded his gun. He gave Johnny Black a last look, shook his head in a regretful gesture, mounted and rode away.

VII

The sun was high in the heavens when Buck Duane finally rode back into town and toward Finley's big white house. He opened a gate and walked in after tying Bullet to a hitching post, knocked on the door. His knock was answered by Cathy.

"Hello," she greeted him brightly. She was dressed in a blue skirt and blouse and a blue ribbon was tied in her blonde hair. She was beautiful. "Come in," she said, and held the door wide.

"I came to see your uncle," he said.

"I know. He is in the parlor with Tulsa Harrow. They've been expecting you. I was thinking of riding out this afternoon, into the hills. I know a pretty place alongside a stream surrounded by cottonwoods. It's a wonderful place for a small picnic—and things."

She looked up at him for his answer.

"Maybe your uncle wouldn't like that, having a picnic with one of his hired hands. If he hires me, that is."

"Oh, bother that! He lets me do what I want. Well?"

Duane smiled. "All right, if you say so."

"Good. I'll meet you on the hill, where we met yesterday. I'll pack a lunch in a saddlebag."

She led him into the parlor where Finley and Tulsa Harrow sat. The house was in perfect order, the plush furniture expensive and in good taste. It was a home that had known the touch of a woman's hand, a woman of culture. Duane wondered who she might have been, and how a woman like that could have known a man like Jonathan Finley, known him, married him, slept with him.

"Come in, Mr. Duane," Finley said. "Buck, isn't it?"

"Yes, sir."

Finley rose, shook hands with him. Tulsa remained seated. He nodded briefly to Buck. Duane saw that Finley was strangely neat in his dress: boots, trousers, shirt were of the best. The string tie added to his appearance. The silver-handled guns didn't escape his notice either. Finley motioned him to a chair and he sat down.

"Buck," Finley said, "we'd like to know something about you. I've heard you're very fast with those guns. That tells me a lot. Where do you hail from?"

"Galveston. The guns?" He looked from one to the other, saw that Tulsa was gazing at him intently. "I've used them."

"How?" Tulsa asked. There was a twofold meaning in his tone.

"Well, let me put it this way. "I was an outlaw. I—"

"*Was?*" Finley asked.

"Had to leave Galveston. Things got kind of hot for me around there. Haven't done a thing in months. Frankly, I don't know what I want to do. But I'm telling you this so there won't be any kind of misunderstanding."

"I see," Finley said. "You mean in case someone comes

looking for you?''

"They might."

"You met some of the boys yesterday in Osage," Finley said. "You know they're no cowhands, don't you?"

"I figured as much."

"What else did you figure?" Tulsa asked.

Duane gave them a small smile and spread his hands. "I got it they made their living dishonestly."

Finley let out a loud laugh. Tulsa Harrow just stared. It was hard for Duane to tell exactly what Tulsa was thinking.

Finley said, "Tulsa, take him in. I think he's all right."

"I'm not sure, but I hope you are, Duane. If you aren't, you and I will have a little meeting in the street. I'd just like to find out how fast you are with those Colts."

Duane grinned back at him. "It might be interesting at that."

"All right, boys," Finley said. "Let's have none of that. Buck, you're hired. You do just as Tulsa says and you'll get along fine. Now, how are you fixed for money?"

"I have a little."

Finley rose, dug a hand into a pocket of his trousers and counted out some gold. "Here's a hundred dollars. That's on account. I'll deduct it from your pay. What you earn will depend on what you do. I hope we understand one another."

Duane took the coins, put them in a shirt pocket. "I'm sure we do, Mr. Finley."

"Good. I understand you're living at the Widow Crowe's. Is that right?"

"Yes, sir."

"Fine woman. Too bad about her husband. Well," he said then, "I'm sure I don't have to tell you not to discuss anything with her. We like to keep our business private."

"I understand perfectly, Mr. Finley."

"Good, good." He turned to Tulsa. "You have something to tell Buck?"

"Yeah. Stay close to town. Slap will tell you anything I want you to know. There'll be something in the next few days."

"I'll be around."

Tulsa eyed him narrowly. "I don't mind telling you I don't particularly like you. There's something about you don't hit me just right. If you make any wrong moves—"

"That's enough, Tulsa!" Finley said harshly. "He's one of us now and I don't want any ill-feelings between you. All right, Buck, go on. I want to talk to Tulsa."

Buck Duane gave Tulsa a quick sidelong look and went out. He whistled for Bullet who came trotting over, mounted, and rode out to the hill to keep his rendezvous with Cathy. He found her already there when he rode up.

"Let's ride over to the spillways," she said. "I know a quiet place there where no one ever goes."

"Shortly. I want to ask you something. I'm not hankerin' to get in bad with your uncle. He just hired me."

"So? Are you saying you're afraid of my uncle?"

"No."

"Of me?" she asked coquettishly. "Come on," she urged, "I promise not to lead you astray." She paused and eyed him with a mischevious glance, a smile playing around the corners of her mobile mouth. "Unless," she added, "you're willing."

He gave her a short, mirthful laugh. "You might be biting off more than you can chew."

"I've got enough teeth. Let's go."

They rode out, over the hills, through a valley, out where the western slopes and valley stretched for miles, where once buffalo roamed and war parties of Indians had crossed, out where there were no trees and endless grass, where the antelope ran and coyotes slept waiting for the night. They came at last to a running stream.

"This is it," she said, and dismounted. "It's lovely, isn't it?" she cried, and stretched her slim white arms to the sky.

He nodded his head. "Yes, it's really nice. Like a slice of another world. You come here often?"

"Occasionally. When I want to get off by myself." She took hold of his hand. "Come on, let's sit by the stream."

They sat down together, side by side, she leaned her head against his shoulder and they sat there like that for a long time. Suddenly, he put his hand around her waist and pulled her gently down. She gave him no resistance, and when he bent his head over hers, she parted her lips, closed her eyes, and waited for his kiss.

The world beyond was shut out, walled off, a planet millions of miles from their own little planet with its own sun, its slice of blue sky, a murmuring stream, and between them no space, and over them no time. They had reached a compromise with a union as old as the ages. He wanted her, as much, no doubt, as she wanted him.

But Buck Duane had held back, contenting himself with the sweetness of her lips and the thrilling closeness of her young body, the warmth of it, the softness, the way she turned in his arms, snuggled against his chest. Cathy was so young, so terribly young and virginal, so gifted with the precious jewels a woman's love could bestow.

They lay on their backs now, eyes closed. There was a dreamy expression on Cathy's face, and her lips were pursed in a faint pout. She reached out a hand, found one of his and held it.

"Why not, Buck?" she asked in a plaintive tone. "Don't you find me attractive?"

"Sure, Cathy. But it wouldn't be right. Not for you, and well, not for me either. I can't explain why."

She didn't understand entirely. She didn't understand that what he couldn't tell her was that he was in Tafton to break up her uncle's gang, to break it up, arrest him, and perhaps even have to kill him. That would hurt her. It was enough. He couldn't hurt her more by deceiving her entirely.

What bothered him was the question of how much she knew of her uncle's life? If she did know, the truth, that is, did she accept it and condone it? Approve it? Or turn her mind away from it and ignore it because she was tied to Jonathan Finley by blood, duty, debt, and and affection a daughter might have for a doting father, for he was more like her father than he was her uncle. It was more difficult, he thought, to understand a woman than to love her.

Cathy opened her eyes suddenly, turned her head and gazed at Buck, studied him for a long time, his every feature, the fine forehead, straight nose, strong mouth and jaw, and the long lashes covering his closed eyes. He was very handsome, she thought. She nudged him with her elbow and he opened his eyes.

"Thinking?" she asked.

He stretched his arms to the sky and then forward toward the sinking sun. "A little."

With feminine logic, she said, "About me? You were, weren't you?"

"Yes, I was."

Her blue eyes reflected a great gentleness and tenderness. She thought, perhaps, that here at last was the man her young-girl dreams had conjured, the lover, the husband to help her by love, passion, the bright and desperate taking and giving that was like liquid velvet coursing through her veins. She thrust herself into his arms.

"Hold me, Buck," Cathy whispered. "Hold me tight. I love you, Buck. Don't ever let me go. Don't ever let anything happen to you."

Duane realized that she had been washed over with a great emotion too much for her to bear alone and that she needed him to damn it up yet contain it and at the same time release her from the panic it wrought in her.

He held her to him tightly for a long time, and when, at last, the sun threatened to sink into the horizon, he took his arms from around her.

"I think we should be getting back, Cathy. Your uncle will be wondering what happened to you." He stood up, held out a hand to her and lifted her to her feet.

They rode back in lighthearted silence and when they reached the edge of the hill where they had met, he said, "I think you should ride on ahead. I'll take the north path around your house and ride home so I won't have to pass the Osage."

Cathy moved her horse close to his, leaned over for a kiss. And then another. "Tomorrow," she threw at him as she spurred her horse. "Same place. Same time."

He watched her ride, marveled at her horsemanship, and then turned Bullet's head and headed for home.

47

VIII

Buck Duane rode into the large back yard behind Abby Crowe's house, and made it without anyone seeing him. He unsaddled Bullet and put him in the barn then walked into the house. There was a tantalizing aroma of food cooking—roast meat, vegetables, and fresh-baked bread. It transmitted itself to him in such a way that he became immediately hungry.

Duane inhaled the aromas several times before stepping into the kitchen, and wondered where he would eat. The afternoon's riding and the hours with Cathy Finley had sharpened his hunger. Abby was in the kitchen, standing over the stove and stirring something in the pot.

"Hello," she greeted him brightly. "You look like you've been out in the sun."

"Yes," he answered lightly. "I rode out into the hills a ways. I like doing that, getting off by myself at times." He was very close to her. She smelled clean, as if she had bathed only a short time ago. There was a subtle scent of jasmine about her.

Duane said, in a small-boyish way, "You smell pretty. Like flowers touched with early morning dew."

Abby turned her head sharply and stared at him in wonder and then her face broke into a bright smile. "Well!" she replied. "I do declare, Buck, that's the nicest thing that's been said to me in years. I'll repay that by asking you to share my supper. I hope you're hungry."

"I shouldn't ought to. That wood costs a lot; and after all, you have to work for it."

"I won't hear another word about that, Buck. Now you go wash up and get ready." Abby looked up into his eyes, and her intuition told her he had been out with a woman during the afternoon. She felt a sharp pang of jealousy.

She shook it off and said, "You know, Buck, one of the great pleasures a woman has is cooking for some man. And I haven't had that pleasure for a long time. Would you deprive me of that?"

"I wouldn't deprive you of anything you wanted, Abby," he said. "I think you're one of the nicest persons I've ever known."

They stood there in silence for a while, gazing at each other awkwardly, each with his own personal thoughts although they were miles apart in what they were thinking.

"All right, then," Abby said, and her tone was that of a wife talking to her husband, "you go and wash up. Bring in fresh water from the well. Here's the pail."

Duane went out to the well, pumped the pail full of water and brought it in. While he was out, the picture of his having been with another woman assailed Abby and tortured her. She knew she had no right to those thoughts, that he had said nothing or done anything to encourage her feeling about him. That she had feelings about him she couldn't deny.

She brushed an errant wisp of hair from her forehead, noted that her face was suddenly damp, and wiped it quickly with a dab of the towel she held in her hand.

When Buck Duane came in she turned to look at him in a swift gaze she felt her pulse hammering, along the lines of her throat, her forehead, and at her wrists.

"Take the pan out on the back porch," Abby said without turning around. There's soap and a fresh towel in the cupboard." She pointed to the cupboard over her head.

He reached up to get the soap and towel and inadvertently leaned against her. She turned swiftly, and as swiftly was in his arms, her head on his chest, her arms around his waist.

"I can't help it," Abby moaned, "I can't help it. Just hold me for a little while," she pleaded. "Please, please, hold me."

Duane held her, understanding the problem that was buried deep within her, the frustration, the lost and wasted years of her life alone since her husband was killed. But he couldn't get involved, and he couldn't let her get involved with him. It wouldn't be fair to her.

Abby remained in Duane's arms for a long time and then she looked up at him with misty eyes, a toilsome hungering within them, shadowed, burning, fading, glowing brightly as she fought her feeling or gave way to them.

"I'm all right," she said at last. "That was foolish of me, I know," she said in an embarrassed tone. "Forgive me." She turned abruptly away from him but he put his hands on her shoulders and spun her around gently.

"It wasn't foolish, Abby. There was nothing foolish about it. I understand. I've been lonely many times, wanting someone to talk to, someone to look at, a friendly face, a man, a woman, especially a woman. But out there in the hills or the plains there was nothing but the night and the howling of coyotes. I know what it is to be lonely. Don't be sorry for what you did. I'm glad you did."

She looked up at him with great tenderness in her eyes. "Are you really, Buck? Really glad?"

"Yes, I am," he answered truthfully.

"Thank you," she said softly. "It helps a great deal. Now," she said briskly in a sudden change of tone, "go on and sit down and I'll serve our suppe

Duane met Cathy the next afternoon at the top of the hill and they rode out to the same place where they had spent the hours the day before. He saw things this afternoon he hadn't observed yesterday. There were mesquite flats along the trails, some of them broken by tenacious cedars, red sandstone canyons, and in the brassy haze of the boundless plains, scattered cattle outfits which held only small herds.

The Ranger believed that Jonathan Finly was responsible for what he saw. He envisioned the broken hopes, the despair, the shattered emotions, the desperate struggles against a hardened villainy and the guns of hired killers who were backed by the power and the law contained in a single man. His absorption in his thoughts irked Cathy.

"Buck, say something! You haven't said a word in five miles! I'm *here*, Buck," she said peevishly and in a mocking tone. "See?"

He turned to her and smiled, "Sure, Cathy. I've just been thinking a little is all."

"About me, I hope. You aren't shilly-shallying around

with the Widow Crowe, are you?" It was said in a teasing tone, but there was a mild challenge in her voice.

"No, Cathy. One woman at a time. You're all I can handle."

"Come on then!" she shouted, and spurred her horse.

They reached over the hills and the valleys, running at breakneck speed. Her superb horsemanship forced him to exercise all his skill to keep up with her. They came at last to the stream, dismounted, shooed their horses away, and flopped down on the grass, exhausted and laughing. Cathy stretched her arms toward the bright sky.

"It's wonderful, Buck. Everything's wonderful. The whole world is wonderful." She turned to him. "And you," she whispered, "are the most wonderful." She sighed and went into his arms.

Cathy Finley was so young, he thought for the second time. So young and enthusiastic. So full of dreams, romance, the springtime of love. It ennobled her in a way, created life out of life, spirit out of spirit, contained her, sailed her into a new world, a new adventure each day, each hour, each minute.

"You're very beautiful, Cathy," he said softly, and caressed her hair with tender fingers.

She murmured words he couldn't hear, soft words trailing off into a misty atmosphere beyond where they lay. It was as if she were talking to herself, which she most likely was, personalizing this idyllic splendor, cherishing, nurturing it, possessing him in this moment of quietude more than he ever could possess her.

She traced a finger up and down his chest, moved closer to him, sighed, closed her eyes and let the world around her vanish into a void, and suddenly she was alone with him in the small planet no one else could reach.

Riding back to town he was silent again, thinking in terms of the incongruity at the magnificence of her youth, her obvious affection, the explosive manner in which she reacted in their intimate moments though they remained innocent in character. She was still in her teens, in the last year of them, of course, but she was a woman in every sense, mature and sophisticated.

IX

Jonathan Finley's day of using a gun were over, but he had transferred them to the gang he used for his depredations and raids around the countryside.

Duane had been unable to learn anything about Cathy's father. He asked Abby about him in a discreet way, but she knew nothing of him.

"There have been rumors from time to time from the folks in the territory that he had been involved with some outlaws, with men like Wesley Hardin, Doc Holliday, and Johnny Ringo. But these, too, were just rumors. No one really knows for a certainty."

"I see," he said reflectively.

"It is important that you know, Buck?"

"No, not too important."

He asked Jeff Kelly about it but he, too, knew nothing other than information he had heard at church picnics or when the men got together at roundup time. Hiram Callahan, the owner of the general store, although he had been in Tafton for years, knew no more. Someone in the Osage hinted that Morris Finley had been hanged as a rustler. It wasn't hard to believe. If that were true then he could understand why Cathy wouldn't talk about him.

One thing that troubled the Ranger most now, ten days after he had arrived in town, was why he hadn't been included in the raid the gang had made on a small bank twenty miles away. Another sore question was what Cathy would do when Captain MacNelly and his men came to arrest her uncle.

Duane did not understand her for a moment. He was certain she would consider him a traitor of the worst sort, of having used her shamelessly, leading her on, accepting her affection only to destroy her only living relative and her along with him. The Ranger visualized the anger that would possess her. Well, it was too late to break off with Cathy now. Perhaps he had been foolish in taking up with her in the first place.

Duane didn't think, however, that it would go on as it had. When they continued seeing each other, there was no stopping it. Duane cursed himself for a fool and wondered what Captain MacNelly would have to say about it. Probably nothing. All MacNelly was interested in was the breakup of the gang. How Duane did it was his business. He could almost hear MacNelly said, "All's fair in love and war, Buck. Hope you enjoyed it."

Buck Duane tried to shrug off the involvement and its potential consequences, but a sense of guilt assailed him. The long corridor of his honesty since the day when he had given up being an outlaw suddenly became murky in his mind. He had been untrue to himself, false to the code by which he had chosen to live. Duane wondered what Jeff and Sara Kelly would think about it when they found out. And Abby.

The Ranger came to a quick awareness of the fact that he cared what the Kellys would think, but most of all what Abby would think. She knew him so slightly and yet trusted him so much. She had been torn on the jagged edges of life by the violent death of her husband. It was unfair to betray her confidence in him.

Two weeks later Duane was in the Osage and Slap Wilson said, "I got a message for you, Buck. Mr. Finley and Tulsa, they want to see us at Mr. Finley's house at two o'clock this afternoon. I was agoin' to ride over to the Widow Crowe's house to tell you but you saved me the trouble. It's 'bout that time now. Let's go."

They rode to the big white house, paused at the wide gate. Wilson reached down from his horse and unhooked the gate and they rode in, dismounted behind the house, tied their horses. A Mexican maid, young, pretty, opened the door for them.

"Buenas tardes. El Senor Finley los esta esperando en la biblioteca. Pasen." She held the door wide and they entered.

"What'd she say?" Slap asked.

"Mr. Finley is in the library. He's expecting us."

"You speak Mex?"

"A little. She spoke Spanish. Excellent Spanish."

"Yeah? What you know! I thought all them Mex were dumb."

"Their culture is older than ours." The Ranger grinned without humor.

In the library they found Finley and Tulsa Harrow sitting in large armchairs smoking cigars. Neither man rose.

"Come in, boys," Finley said. "Take chairs."

They sat down opposite Finley and Tulsa. Duane noted something about Jonathan Finley that had escaped him in their previous meeting. The thin, grudging line that was his mouth. There was cruelty there, as there was in the suspicious clear blue eyes.

Finley said, "Buck, I'm sure you know all about our operations by now. We figured we would give you enough time to think about it, even to ask around a little. I'm sure you have. If you haven't, then I've underestimated you."

Duane nodded his head.

Tulsa leaned back in his chair, took a long puff from his cigar, then leaned forward, the cigar in his hand, pointing it at Duane as he spoke.

"Duane, I've tried to figure you from the beginning. Maybe I have and maybe I haven't. I thought at first you might be a saddle tramp, but changed my mind when I thought of your guns. Bounty hunter? No. I couldn't figure you for that either, although you may be just sneaky enough to be one."

There was a sudden silence in the room, heavy, awkward, and threatening to burst into violence. Duane didn't move a muscle, just sat and stared at Tulsa.

"I said to myself," Tulsa went on, "what the hell is he? I did a little checking. I know about your old man. Got the word from Abilene. Ever been in Abilene, Duane?"

"Nope."

"Ever know a man named Bill Longley?"

"Nope."

"Cheseldine?"

"I've heard of him."

"That's all?"

"That's all."

"How about Captain MacNelly?"

"He tracked me for a long time."

Tulsa eyed him narrowly. "He's head of the Texas Rangers. A tough lawman, they say."

"So I've heard." Duaned paused a moment. "He never lets up."

Tulsa sneered. "MacNelly couldn't find a prayer in a Bible. All right, Duane. I've said my piece. You know exactly what I was fishing for. Don't make any wrong moves."

"You said that once before."

"I'm saying it again. Keep it in mind."

Finley and Tulsa exchanged glances of complete understanding. It was a swift, gliding gesture but they had told each other something which, if spoken, would have taken a thousand words. These two, Duane thought, were models for the old saying, *Thick as thieves*.

The Ranger gave a slight, noncommital shrug and told himself that whatever passed between them didn't matter a damn to him. Unless, if he made a wrong move, they decided to shoot him in the back. He doubted this. Egoist that Tulsa was, with an overbearing pride and confidence in his ability to beat any man alive to the draw, he would want to meet Duane in the middle of Main Street, at high noon, and with the whole town gathered there to witness his performance. That suited Buck Duance just fine.

Jonathan Finley rose from his chair. "All right, Duane. I think you understand Tulsa, and that means you understand me, too. We have to be careful. We have to choose our men with caution. You did me a good turn by saving my life. I'm paying it back by giving you a chance to make more money than you ever made in your life. This is your first opportunity."

Finley nodded to Tulsa Harrow and Slap Wilson. They rose and went to a long narrow table where Finley spread a map. He pointed to a small circle on the map.

"This, gentlemen, is the town of Hope. It's near the Del Rio-El Paso supply road. Used to be Comanche country but the redskins ceased to threaten the territory years ago. It's a very thriving town with big spreads all around. The ranchers use the bank to deposit their money after they sell their cattle. I have the word that something like thirty to fourty thousand dollars will be in the bank next week. I figure it to be Tuesday.

"There's only three people in the bank. Man by the name of Colby owns it. He'll be there. Always is. He's a big man. Over six feet, with thick black hair and bushy eyebrows. Can't mistake him. Most of the money will be in the safe. He's the only one has the combination, so don't bother with the other two. Don't give Colby a chance to go for a gun. He has several under the counter and is known to use them.

"The town has all the usual shops, and four saloons. The bank is between the general store and a saloon known as the M & M. It's run by two men known as Tony McCrann and Mario Lubichek, a couple of wild men out of Deadwood, big and fast. They kinda look after things in town because there isn't a sheriff there. Watch these two. They're dangerous.

"When you ride in, have half your men go into the saloon, Tulsa. Post one man at the door to give the signal for them to leave after you take the bank. But don't let Tony or Mario get the drop on your men. This here—" he pointed to a black pencil line—"is how you come back. It's hilly country and offers a lot of protection just in case they form a posse."

The three men followed the pencil line, took in the towns and the marked-off trails. Duane knew the territory well. So did the other two, and said so.

"You decide who goes into the bank with you, Tulsa."

"I already have. Slap and Duane."

Harrow looked hard at Duane. "Any objections?"

"None at all. That's what I'm here for."

"Good," Finley said. "I suggest you leave tomorrow morning. That will get you into Hope Tuesday in plenty of time. That's all, gentlemen. Good luck."

As they started to leave, Finley said, "Tulsa, you stay a minute. Want to talk to you."

Duane and Slap Wilson walked through the kitchen and were let out by the Mexican maid, who smiled shyly at

Duane. He said something to her in Spanish and she laughed, thanked him and closed the door behind him.

When they rode out the gate, Slap Wilson turned his horse's head toward the Osage. "You comin' with me, Buck?"

"Don't think so, Slap. I want to get some stuff together for the trip."

"What's there to take? All you need is your bedroll."

"Sure, but I want to rest my horse, clean my guns, things like that."

"'Course. Well, I'll just mosey over to the Osage and tell the rest of the boys to be ready. We'll leave at sunup. Meet at the Osage. Get a good rest and clean those guns good."

"I will."

X

Abby had bathed an hour before Duane left Jonathan Finley's house. She thought deeply all the time she was in the big tub, and told herself with quiet resignation that she had no chance with Duane at all, or at best a very small chance. Yet she was helpless before him. His very presence unnerved her so that she could barely breathe at times. When he passed close to her she trembled as with a sudden attack of ague and her legs turned to water.

Buck Duane had brought her great distress, made her feel inadequate, less a woman, yet if he weren't there she couldn't bear it. With hope in her heart, she told herself that perhaps time would play in her favor. This was her secret. She held it within her because she was proper, prim, even—to all outside appearances, that is. The morality to which she held, which restrained her from throwing herself at him, was what she couldn't deny. It was like a form of religion.

Yet she argued with herself, a moral significance which held within itself a tragic consequence, which harbored loneliness and physical hunger, couldn't be entirely right. The meaning of her life was spinning away from her.

"Buck!" she cried aloud. "Help me, help me!"

She did odd chores around the house for a while, then went into his room, picked over his clothes to see if they needed mending, or a button sewed on somewhere. She found a shirt that had a tear in one sleeve. She got her sewing basket, sat on his bed and began to repair it. Duane came in just as she finished.

She held up the shirt. "There was a small tear at the elbow. I fixed it. You don't mind, do you?"

"No, Abby, I don't mind. Thank you." He took her by the hand and led her into the kitchen. "Sit down, Abby. I have to talk to you."

He was so grave that it frightened her. Her first thought was that he was leaving and she grew faint at the thought. As always, she repressed her emotions with difficulty. She uttered a silent prayer. "He's not leaving. God, he's not leaving." She sat in a chair and he took one opposite her at the table.

"Abby, when I first came here I asked you to trust me no matter what happened or what you heard."

"But I've heard nothing, Buck. I wouldn't believe it anyway."

"Yes, of course. But I now have to ask for your trust in a different way. I have to trust *you*."

"Oh, Buck, you can trust me with anything. I'll do whatever you say."

"I knew you would. Abby, I'm a special agent, assigned to the Texas Rangers under Captain MacNelly."

She could not hide her astonishment. Her mouth opened and her lips moved wordlessly as she stared at him.

"My job here, Abby, is to wipe out the Finley gang. Tulsa Harrow. Slap Wilson. All the rest."

She found her voice. "My God! You? Alone?"

"Just about."

"But that man Harrow is a devil! A killer. He killed my husband. A score of other men! Oh, Buck, I'm afraid something dreadful will happen to you!"

"No," he replied, and shook his head. "Don't be

afraid. I have to ask you to do something for me."

"Yes, yes, Buck. Anything."

"I'm going to write a note that I want you to take to Mr. Callahan at the general store. Be very sure that no one sees you giving him the note. When you give it to him just say one word. 'Kelly.' He'll understand. While you're there, buy something. Groceries. Anything. Here." He handed her half a dozen silver dollars.

"I have some money, Buck," she protested.

"Take that. It's not one hundredth enough for what you are going to do."

"Oh, Buck, Buck, I don't want to be paid for this. I—"

"I didn't mean it in that way," he broke in. "Go on, honey, get dressed while I write the note. Give me a pencil and paper."

She hurried to get the writing material and shivered as she hastened to a small desk in the living room. Had he meant what he called her, or was it a slip of the tongue? Honey! Abby could scarcely breathe as she came back with the pencil and paper. He took it from her hand and saw that it trembled.

"Are you scared?" Duane asked.

"Oh, no. No. I'd do this a hundred times if it meant that we would at last be rid of those men. I'm not afraid, Buck." She hurried away lest he see the flush that suddenly rose to her cheeks.

Buck Duane wrote:

Hope. Tuesday morning. Bank. No time. Will have to go through with it if you don't make it. May be trouble with posse.

He folded the sheet of paper into a small square. Abby came into the kitchen with a shawl over her shoulders and a market basket under one arm.

"This is the note," Duane said. "Be careful. Don't pass it if you think you'll be seen. It might mean the death of Callahan."

"I'll be careful. Trust me."

"I do trust you," he told her firmly. "Completely." He took told of her arms, held them tightly. She hurt but she didn't make a protest because she felt, for the first time

59

since his coming that he was touched by a realization of her presence as a woman.

"I hate asking you to do this, Abby," Duane finally said. "But I'm sure either Tulsa or one of his men is on the lookout for me, for anything I may do that would betray me. They suspect me. Tulsa does, anyway. That's why I asked you to do this."

He gripped her arms tighter. "But, for God's sake, be careful. Don't let anyone see you hand Callahan the note."

"I won't, Buck. I'll be very careful."

He let go her arms and she stood there looking into his eyes, searchingly. What Abby saw gave her a great lift. She turned and went out the door and into the street, her heart singing.

There were two ladies in the store whom Abby Crowe knew. They greeted each other and spoke of everyday things women talk about. Another woman came in when Callahan had finished waiting on the first two women, and he turned to Abby.

"What would you like today, Mrs. Crowe?"

"Over here, Mr. Callahan. Will you please lift this bolt down for me? I think it's something I want."

He came from behind the counter toward her where she stood behind a counter laden with more goods. Abby looked to see if the woman was watching. She wasn't. She handed Callahan the note in a quick gesture.

"Kelly," she said softly, and watched his expression.

He put the note into a pocket of his trousers without looking at her and said, "Yes, Mrs. Crowe, that's a very fine piece of goods. Cotton. A beautiful pattern."

"So it is, but I think I'll wait until next week. I'd like two steaks. Cut them thick, please."

He bent close to her. "I'll have this to Kelly in an hour, as soon as my old woman comes in," he whispered.

Abby smiled at him and sighed in relief. She bought some fruit, a box of salt, some spices, and a pound of butter, paid her bill, and left with the satisfied feeling that she had accomplished a great deed, something that would help to rid the town of its robbers and killers.

She almost ran home, hurried into the house, put the basket down and cried, "I did it, Buck! No one saw me. Mr. Callahan said Kelly would have the note in an hour!"

She was flushed with excitement of the thing and her dark candid eyes were shining. He reached out his arms and took her in them, and gave her a tight hug.

"Good girl. I'm very relieved."

She was suddenly enveloped with a mixture of feelings, excitement and exhilaration over what she had done, involvement in a conspiracy that had broken up the routine of her life, and concern over what might happen to Buck.

When he released her she said, "I can't help worrying about what may happen to you, Buck. That whole gang. If they should find out—"

He gave her a reassuring smile. "Don't worry about it, Abby. Nothing will happen to me." He lifted her chin. "Just trust me. Everything will turn out all right."

"I hope so. I'll pray for you, for things to go right."

"That'll help," he answered soberly.

"Are you hungry? Would you like me to fix supper now?"

"Not right away. I have a few things to do. How about six o'clock?"

"All right, Buck. Whatever you say."

Duane was up early the next morning, as was Abby. She was in the kitchen busy making his breakfast. They ate in comparative silence, each unwilling to talk about the impending events of the day. When he finished he stood up and looked down at her, wanting to say the right thing but unable to call the right words to his mind.

Abby had been thrown into a sudden and startling void now that he was ready to leave. She, too, groped for something to say but couldn't find the words.

"Well," the Ranger said at last, "I'll be seeing you in about four or five days." He started for the door.

She jumped up from her chair, ran to him as he reached the door. "Buck, be careful," she said in a tormented voice. "Don't let anything happen to you."

"I won't," he said firmly, and gave her an affectionate

pat on her back. "Don't worry about me. I'll be back."

Duane turned then and went out the door. He didn't see her when she bent her head to her hands and burst into tears, her whole body shaking with the sudden breaking of the dam that had held back the surging emotions of her fears.

The Ranger rode out to the Osage, found the gang already gathered in the saloon, all but Tulsa. The gang was boisterous, drinking and yelling, pounding each other on the back, spilling liquor on the bar and calling for more.

Duane had moved to the farthest end of the long bar and nursed a glass of beer. And then Tulsa Harrow came in. He was dressed in tan Oregon pants, a tan shirt and jacket, and tan cowman's boots that had been highly polished. His silver-handled Colts, loose in the two holsters, shook a little as he walked in and stopped just inside the door.

He said nothing for a long time, just stared at the group who quieted down much as a classroom of kids might have done with the sudden appearance of an absent teacher.

"That's all," Tulsa said in a low voice. "I said to meet here, not to meet and drink. If anyone has a hankering to take along a bottle of whiskey, I advise you not to. Let's go."

The words dripped from his mouth like so much acid, and his eyes followed every man as he left the bar and went out the door. When Buck Duane reached him, he said, "I'm hoping you make a wrong move, Duane. I'll be at your back every second. When we reach the bank, you go in first and throw your gun on the guy that owns it."

"Sure, Tulsa. Anything else?"

"Yeah. If he reaches for one of those guns he's got under the counter you better shoot him. If you don't, I'll get you first and then him. We understand each other?"

"Like a couple of lovebirds, Tulsa," Duane snapped and went out the door.

The lush colors of early autumn, gold, green, purple, red, and orange, shone under the rising sun as they rode out of town toward the trail leading to the hills, valleys, and the flatlands that would take them into Hope.

Slap Wilson rode in front, the other ten members of the gang behind him, and behind them, Buck Duane. Bringing up the rear, some twenty feet behind Duane, was Tulsa Harrow. They rode leisurely, paused at a stream to rest and water their horses when the sun was straight over their heads.

To the west of the stream, a row of new poles went straggling away toward a slope; copper wires, gleaming in the sun, sagged from narrow cross-arms. The smell of burning hair and side told them someone was branding cattle or had finished branding them a short while ago. Duane caught Tulsa looking at him intently while he watered Bullet and he stared back without wavering his glance. Both men tired of staring at each other and turned their gaze.

Tulsa waved an arm, yelled, "Let's go!"

The paused again in late afternoon beside another stream, took food from their saddle bags, ate, dipped hands into the stream and washed their dust-covered faces, then scooped up water into their hands and quenched their thirst.

By dusk they had reached a flat stretch of ground beyond which was a row of ragged hills, and in the middle of the ground a narrow stream ran between a thicket of scrub-oak. Beyond the trees, on the far side of the stream, brush grew thick and tall.

Tulsa yelled to the gang to halt. He rode up to their midst, said, "We'll camp here for the night. Stu, pick up some branches or stray logs for a fire. We'll make some coffee."

The gang dismounted, unsaddled their horses. Most of them led the animals to the stream for a drink and then turned them loose to feed on the grass. Duane led Bullet to the stream, watered him, then led him back to a tall patch of grass where he could feed to his heart's content.

Night fell swiftly, the darkness hemming them in but for the glow of the camp-fire and the faint light of the silver moon that hung low in the sky. Duane found a place against a tree a short distance from the camp-fire around which the rest of the gang had formed a circle and leaned against it. He sat there for a long time with his thoughts and wondered if Captain MacNelly would get his message in time, and getting it, if he would be able to notify sheriffs in towns surrounding Hope in time to stop the holdup and the murder of the owner of the bank.

The Ranger was sure that Tulsa intended to kill him the moment they entered the bank. Duane knew he wouldn't have a chance to kill both Tulsa and Slap. If he shot Tulsa then Slap would surely kill him. The thought of having to shoot the owner of the bank troubled him. This wasn't in the plan at all. But how to avoid it? That was the problem.

Duane got up, stretched, and headed for the stream, bent down and threw water on his face and over his hair, took a long drink, rose, wiped his face and hair with a bandana, and started across the stream toward a hill. He had expected Tulsa to stop him, yell at him, ask him where he was going, but he didn't. He waded across the stream, the water coming to just over his ankles, the boots keeping his feet dry, and made his way up the hill.

He walked to the outer edge on the farther side, saw a declivity that formed one side of a gully. There was a tangle of wild, virginal growth in the bottom of the gully, and then a long, gradual slope that led to some timber. Behind the timber was a small ranch house. A light shone in one of the windows facing him.

Duance raced down the slope of the hill and ran toward the house. He knocked on the door and a tall, slim man in his late twenties, bronzed, with wide shoulders and slim hips which told of years in the saddle, stood framed in the doorway.

"What is it, stranger?"

"I have to talk to you," Duane said. "It's important."

The urgency in Duane's voice struck through to the

man. He held the door back for Duane to enter. A tall, graceful young woman, with the copper-hued skin of an Indian or a half-breed, came out from the kitchen, stood there and gazed first at Duane and then at her husband.

"What is it, Josh?" she asked in a nervous tone.

"A stranger, Yolanda, who needs help."

"I'm sorry if I frightened you, Ma'am," Duane said, "but I need help." He looked from one to the other, decided he could trust them. "I'm a Texas Ranger. I joined a gang to break them up. They're going to rob the bank in Hope."

The woman turned pale, put both hands to her face. "Ohhh—"

"Why did you come here?" the man asked.

"How far is Hope from here?"

"About twenty miles."

"I must ask you to ride in tonight. Get to the owner of the bank and warn him. Tell him who I am. Tell him I'll be wearing a red bandana around my neck, that I'll be the first one in the bank, not to shoot me but to protect himself against the other two men when we come into the bank."

The man looked bewildered.

"How will I tell him to do that? Besides, it's dark. The trails are treacherous. It would man forty miles of riding, there and back. It would mean leaving my wife alone. I can't do it. There's no way."

"A man may be killed. Maybe two, three or four. Don't you understand? You have to do it! I can't stay any longer. What's your name?"

"Lerner. Josh Lerner."

"All right, Mr. Lerner. You can make it up and back in four hours, be back shortly after midnight. I have to go. I'm depending on you."

As Duane reached the door, the man yelled at him, "I can't do it!"

Duane didn't wait to argue but ran back as fast as he could, to the top of the hill, across the stream, slowed down, took several deep breaths and walked slowly to the tree where he had left his bedroll. As he was unrolling it,

Tulsa walked up.

"You walk around at night, Duane?"

Buck Duane looked up. "Sometimes," he answered slowly. "I was a little stiff from the day's riding and thought I'd take a walk to loosen my legs. Why?"

"I'll ask the questions, Duane," Tulsa retorted coldly. "From now on you stay put with the rest of the boys. I'll tell you when to go, and where. Understand?"

"Perfectly."

"That's good for you," Tulsa said meaningly, and walked away.

Duane finished unrolling his bedroll, wrapped himself in the blanket and tried to sleep but couldn't. He believed that he had made clear to Josh Lerner the urgency of the situation. If he was any kind of man at all, he would ride out to Hope and warn the owner of the bank.

On the other hand, Duane thought, it might have been a very foolish move. If Tulsa suspected anything—and he was just the kind who would, especially where Duane was concerned—then he might take a walk up the hill and have a look. That look would reveal the ranch house. Lerner struck him as a man who would first want to protect his wife, and himself, and if Tulsa threatened the woman first then surely Lerner would reveal their conversation.

All the work Duane had done so far would be lost. Moreover, Tulsa and Slap would decide to kill him and throw his body into the thick brush where he would never be found. It was an irritating thought, and the Ranger cursed himself for having given in to the impulse to reveal himself to Lerner and his wife. He tossed around for a long time and finally fell into a troubled sleep.

Just before daybreak, Duane felt a boot against his back, turned and looked up into Tulsa's grim face. "Get up, Duane."

Duane moved around under the blanket he had wrapped around himself, every sense alert to Tulsa's manner. All he could determine was that Tulsa's tone held no more animosity toward him than it usually did. But that was his way. He had never raised his voice in all the times that

Duane had talked with him. He hadn't raised his voice when he had talked to Jeff Kelly, but the threat in it had been unmistakable.

The Ranger peered through the haziness of the early morning darkness up at Tulsa's face, at the cold gray eyes that were barely visible to him, so that it was difficult for him to tell exactly what lay behind them. He reached a hand to his gun and unrolled slowly from the blanket, stood up with his right side away from Tulsa. He reached down, picked up the blanket, and held it in such a way that Tulsa could not see the right hand that held the gun half-drawn from its holster.

"You have a funny way of waking up a man," he said with mild irritation. "I don't like a man using a boot on me. You wanted to wake me, all you had to do was call my name. I sleep with my mind half open. I'd have heard you."

Tulsa Harrow stared at him for a long, hard minute. "You'll get used to me after a time, Duane," Tulsa said in that even tone. "Most men do. If they live long enough."

"I'll live long enough," Duane retorted, "but I won't ever get used to you, Tulsa. There's a lot about you that gripes me as much as I gripe you."

Tulsa grunted on a low note. "We'll settle that some day," Tulsa retorted, and snapped off the words. "Right now, get yourself together. We're moving out. Hard riding. We have to be in Hope by nine o'clock."

He turned away from him without another word and strode toward the group, all of whom were up and saddling their horses.

Duane walked to the stream, washed his face, took a long drink, and whistled for Bullet. So Tulsa hadn't gone to see the Lerners. Now, if Josh Lerner had ridden into Hope to warn the banker of the impending robbery, all would come off well. If he hadn't, then everything depended on Jeff Kelly having been able to send off the message to Captain MacNelly in time for MacNelly to warn someone in Hope. Duane saddled and mounted Bullet.

They rode out onto the trail single file, Slap Wilson

leading the way and Tulsa Harrow bringing up the rear. The fore-running glow of the sunrise in the east touched the emerald green of the trail's lush growth, and the fragrant moisture of the morning air poured into Duane's lungs as he rode along breathing in deeply. Light came suddenly and Tulsa yelled to ride hard.

Duane would have been dismayed if he had known how completely Tulsa Harrow's suspicion of him had jelled into certainty. He would have been more dismayed if he had known that Tulsa meant to kill him immediately after they walked out of the bank with the money. The crystallization of Tulsa's suspicions into firm belief that he was other than what he represented himself to be, and possibly a lawman, had persuaded him to kill Duane.

Harrow couldn't do it before the eyes of the gang without provocation because even they, under the code of the West, would have held him low and jeopardized his position as leader. But, coming out of the bank, and under the pretext of shooting at defenders of the town, Tulsa could get away with it.

XII

The gang reached Hope shortly after eight o'clock. It was a town weaned on gunsmoke and death. The M & M Saloon had seen a hundred gunfights and as many killings, and the owners, Tony and Mario, had been involved in a dozen of them. This was something Finley had neglected to say, and only because he hadn't been informed of it by the man who had given him his information on Hope.

Tulsa Harrow yelled a signal and the gang halted on the outskirts of town. He waved a hand and they dismounted as he rode up.

"It's too early to ride in," Tulsa said. "Rest your horses and yourselves. We may have a hard ride out of town and you'll need a fresh horse under you."

Harrow looked the gang over, gave each one instructions. "Slap, Duane, and I will go into the bank. Stu, you stay just outside the door of the saloon, Tony and Mario's, and give the rest of the boys the signal to leave when you see us come out. Bob and Harry, you two kind of mosey around in front of the saloon and have your rifles with you, just in case.

"The rest of you go into the saloon and take care of those two bad men, Tony and Mario if they start trouble. All right, that's it. Lie down and rest."

At ten minutes of nine, Tulsa gave a signal and the men who were to go into the saloon got up from the ground, mounted, and rode slowly into town. They dismounted in front of the saloon, tied their horses to the hitching post with slip knots and went in. The saloon was filled with about twenty cowpokes, all armed. They were drinking beer. There wasn't a bottle of whiskey on the bar. The gang did not notice this highly unusual circumstance.

Five minutes later, Stu rode in, tied his horse, and sat down on a wooden bench to the right of the entrance to the saloon. His rifle was across his lap. Bob and Harry rode up then, tied their horses, and split up, taking positions about fifteen feet from the saloon, looking up and down the street, across the street, and along the side of the street where the saloon was situated.

It struck Bob as odd that not a single soul was on the street. The stores were closed. Shades were drawn behind each window. The only noise audible came from the interior of the saloon. At that moment, Slap, Duane, and Tulsa rode up before the bank and tied their horses to the hitching post.

Tulsa looked around, up and down the street, and motioned to Bob and Harry to be ready in case of trouble. The two men moved to their positions about ten feet from the entrance to the saloon, one on either side.

"All right, Duane," Tulsa said, "this is it. This is where I find out if you're with us or a dog. If you're a dog, you're goin' to die like one. Let's go."

Duane looked up and down the street hoping for a sign that would tell him Captain MacNelly had received Jeff Kelly's telegram. He was certain that Josh Lerner had not ridden into town to warn the banker. That poor young man was scared to death. Well, he couldn't blame him. Why get mixed up in an affair like this? It was none of his business. Besides, he had his wife to think of.

"What's the matter, Duane?" Tulsa sneered. "Got cold feet?"

"I'm just wondering whether you have," Duane retorted. "You wanted me to go in first. Again, I don't like you at my back."

As he spoke the Ranger was bleakly sure that his plans for breaking up the gang had been shot full of holes.

Tulsa drew one of his silver-handled Colts. "Move in, Duane, or I'll drop you right here. In the back. I've never shot a man in the back in my life but I'm willing to make an exception in your case. Let's go."

Duane moved toward the door of the bank. He took a last quick look up and down the street. It was hopeless. No one was about. He drew his gun, pushed open the door, and stepped in. Tulsa Harrow and Slap Wilson followed him.

"Raise your hands!" Duane ordered. "This is a holdup. Raise 'em and you won't get hurt. All we want is the money!"

Tulsa swore. Duane didn't know why in the instant that Tulsa uttered his curse, and then he saw why. The owner was not in the bank. The only ones behind the narrow counter were the two clerks, both of whom now held their hands high in the air.

"There isn't any money here," the smaller of the two clerks said in a quavering voice. "Mr. Colby was in early this morning and took all the money to Walden."

Tulsa's eyes narrowed and his face was blue with anger. It was the first time Duane had seen him lose control.

"Come out here, you!" Tulsa said to the clerk. "Come out!"

The clerk came out from behind the counter, his hands still in the air only now he was shaking with fright as he approached Tulsa.

"Who warned Colby about a holdup?" he demanded. "Talk!"

"I don't know anything, Mister. Honestly. I—"

Tulsa slapped the man across the face—hard. The blow sent the slight man sprawling. Tulsa pointed the gun at him.

"Talk or I'll kill you!"

The man began to blubber. "I don't know anything," he cried in stammering tones. "Please don't kill me. Mr. Colby told us nothing."

Slap Wilson yelled, "Kill him! He's lyin'. I'll kill this other coyote!"

The Ranger had no chance to stop Wilson. The gun in Slap's hand exploded. The clerk behind the counter toppled over. Duane saw the rush of blood that swam over the hapless man's face before he fell. He saw the pale blue smoke drift slowly up from the muzzle of Slap's gun.

There was a haunting stillness for a quick moment as Duane fought indecisively with himself. His first reaction was to shoot Slap but he saw Tulsa's eyes on him and he changed his mind. All this flashed through his thoughts with the speed of light.

"Let's get out of here," he said.

It was the weakest thing he could have said, but it was all he could think of at the moment through the deep, keen disappointment over the turn of events. Slap's features, hard, tough, his ugly mouth twisted into a snarl, his beady eyes fixed on Duane were a shade less in harshness than the look on Tulsa's face.

Duane was certain Tulsa wanted to gun him down there and then but the gun in Duane's hand must have changed his mind. A gunfight here would gain Tulsa nothing.

Suddenly there was the sound of gunfire in the street, a staccato of pistols and rifles. Tulsa and Slap hurried out, and Duane followed them. Stu and Harry lay dead on the wooden walk outside the saloon. Bob had backed off the walk and was firing into the saloon with his rifle, the Winchester smoking as he triggered shot after shot in rigid fire.

Tulsa and Slap screamed oaths, and both ran toward the spot where Bob stood and began firing into the saloon. Shouts from inside the saloon mixed with the sound of the gunfire. Moses Pratt, one of the gang, stumbled out into the street. He was bleeding badly.

"Ambush!" he managed to say in a half-croaking sound and spat up blood. "Too many guns. Run for it!" He coughed up more blood and then collapsed to the ground. He was dead.

Duane raised his Colt, somewhat sickened. Tulsa and Slap were perfect targets—two shots, and the men who were on the point of killing him seconds ago would be dead. But it would not be a lawman's victory, or even a gunfighter's, and it went against the grain. Yet even now they were sending lead into the saloon, perhaps killing the town's defenders while he hesitated.

He leved the .45 at Tulsa—then a searing pain in his arm blended with a thunderclap of sound; the Colt spun from his fingers and he staggered forward.

"Hold it right there!" a voice rasped behind him. "This buffalo gun's got two barrels, and th' second one's trained right on yer kidney."

Duane turned to face a wizened figure clad in rank buckskins, grizzled of hair and beard. Old though he was, the hands that held the massive, ancient weapon were steady, and the Ranger had no reason to doubt the asserted destination of its remaining round.

"Listen, old-timer," he said, "I'm not—"

"Old-timer, is it? I'm about forty years older 'n you're ever goin' to get to be, without you raise yer hands jest as high's they'll go," his captor retorted indignantly. "Rights, I should drop ye where y'are, but I'd kind of like to keep y'alive long enough to tell folks how I got me a bandit. Not much longer'n that, though," he added, wanting to be fair.

Duane raged as he heard the sounds of battle die away behind him. The short, fierce fight was over. He risked a backward glance and saw Slap and Tulsa pounding off down the dusty street, unhit by the following fire from the townspeople.

"I'm a Texas Ranger," he said desperately.

"An' I'm the mighty Yeller Hand, feared sachem of the Pawnee," said the ancient cordially. "Which I eats Texas

Rangers for breakfast, 'specially when I catch 'em robbin' banks. Hey," he called to the townspeople now hurrying up from the saloon, "here's an owlhoot with gumption. Caught him blazin' away at the saloon, then he says he's a Texas Ranger. Knocked the gun outen his hand with the neatest shot I ever—"

"I am a Ranger," Duane grated. "And I'd have got those two killers if it hadn't been for that 'neat shot'!"

"I don't know that he's a Ranger," a voice spoke up. "But I do know he's the man who warned me about the raid and did it strong enough so I rode twenty miles here and gave you people time to set up that ambush!"

Duane's heart leaped up as he saw Josh Lerner. So his gamble on the young rancher's nerve had paid off!

Within minutes, the superficial graze on his arm had been bandaged and he was once again astride Bullet and headed out of Hope, followed by the old hunter's mingled apologies and insistences that it had, after all, been a damn' neat shot.

Tulsa and Wilson were on horses as fresh as his, and they knew the route back to Tafton better; Duane had no illusions about overtaking them. Duane and Bullet covered the miles steadily, but without urgency. The drama was approaching its end, and the last act had to be played at Tafton. Slap and Tulsa would be waiting for him there, and so would Jonathan Finley—and Cathy.

Finley: a tricky proposition. Buck Duane had been sent on his undercover mission to bring the ringleader of the robberies to justice, not to gun him down. Either way, the threat Finley represented would be over; but a live Jonathan Finley, standing trial and getting a fair verdict from a jury meant a lot more to law and to the Rangers than a gray-haired corpse leaking blood into the dust of Main Street.

Finley would be tough to take, but somehow or other, Duane would have to find a way to arrest him and bring him safely to jail. It could be done—maybe.

Cathy: sorrow was what Buck Duane felt mostly. He had disturbed her life, and his own. He had come out of nowhere, given her a dream, and, within a day at the most, would explode that dream and shatter the very fabric of her life. He shouldn't have let himself get involved with the girl—but not often did any man, let alone one whose life was set in the harsh but haunting open spaces, encounter such a woman.

"She has grit," he told himself. "She'll hate me, but maybe that will make it easier for her to take the rest."

Slap Wilson and Tulsa Harrow: death, plain and simple. Duane smiled wryly as he pictured himself telling either, "You're under arrest." As well try to serve a warrant on a cougar! He knew full well that he could have a battery of cannons trained on them at point-blank range, and if he called on them to surrender, they would draw and fire on the gunners.

Yet he also knew that if either were at his back, he would walk safely until the moment they called the challenge. His known prowess with the revolver—and his successful imposture as an outlaw, which had gained him their grudging acceptance—made it necessary for men such as these to face him on their own terms. Unless they shot it out with him, there would be no savor in seeing him dead, no inflation of the one value they cherished, their reputation as gunfighters.

So. . .he would find Slap and Tulsa, or they would find him. And Death would complete the foursome. The only question left was, whose?

And, to something in Buck Duane's deepest self—perhaps a remnant of his outlaw years, perhaps a legacy from his father—the challenge was not entirely unwelcome.

When night fell Buck Duane made camp, and fell into a troubled sleep. When he awoke, the first gray patch of dawn shone in the east. He rose, stretched wearily, walked to where Bullet was tied to a tree, and patted him fondly.

"Hard ride ahead, Boy," Duane said in a low tone. "Got to move." He saddled him, mounted, and rode off, slowly at first because it was still too dark for fast riding.

XIII

Then the sun came up and the sky showed blue. Buck Duane found a spring with a group of cottonwoods beside it. He dismounted and let Bullet drink his fill while he washed his face and quenched his own thirst. He let Bullet graze in the thick grass for about fifteen minutes then mounted him and rode hard. He reached Tafton about ten o'clock and skirted the town, riding directly to Jeff Kelly's spread. He rode in toward the back of the house, dismounted and tied Bullet to a post. As he did so, Jeff Kelly came out of the house.

"I got the message out to Captain MacNelly," he said.

"Good," said Duane.

"Come in, come in, Mr. Duane," Kelly urged.

Duane followed him into the house. Mrs. Kelly was in the kitchen. She appeared excited, trembled a little.

"Would you like some coffee, Mr. Duane? Yes, I think you would. And some breakfast? I'll fix you some breakfast."

"No, thanks. Just some coffee." The Ranger sat down at the table opposite Kelly.

"It's all over town, Mr. Duane. Slap Wilson has been in the Osage the last hour screaming for your blood. He said you got the whole gang killed. All except him and Tulsa Harrow."

Sara Kelly set two cups of coffee before the men. "What will you do, Mr. Duane?" she asked, deep concern in her tone. "Those men will surely kill you."

He shook his head. "Not both at the same time. They'll have to make a fair fight of it. Even Judge Grant, weak as he is, could not chew a killing like that. Two men against one. No. That would be outright murder and I'm sure he knows that if that happened it would blow things sky high. Besides, I think that Tulsa Harrow wants a chance at me first."

He took a swallow from the cup in his hand. "Good coffee, Mrs. Kelly."

"What's the next step, Mr. Duane?" Kelly asked.

"Well, assuming that Tulsa beats me to the draw, I want you to tell Captain MacNelly when he gets here that—"

"Are you sure Captain MacNelly will come? How will he know? All I did was send the message to him about the holdup."

"He'll get the word from Hope about what happened and will know the next step is to come to Tafton and clean things up. As I said, if Tulsa should beat me to the draw before Captain MacNelly gets here I want you to tell him that Jonathan Finley planned this holdup of the bank in my presence, that Slap Wilson killed the bank clerk in Hope. The other clerk will bear witness to that."

"My God!" Mrs. Kelly cried. "I didn't know. Those murderers!"

"I'll tell him all that you've said. Anything else?"

"Yes. I want you to ride out to everyone you know around here and tell him to go into town, move around in the stores and in the street. Tell one and tell him to tell another and those to tell another. That will get most of the people there in about an hour. I'll take it from there."

"I'll do it now."

Both men rose. Duane said, "I have something to take care of first, and then I'll ride into town. I'll give you and your friends an hour."

"I think that's all it will take."

"Good. Thanks for everything. Maybe you'll get a clean town when this is over with." He extended his hand to Kelly who shook it firmly. He turned to Sara Kelly. "Thank you, too." He held out his hand and she took it, tears coursing down her cheeks.

"You're a very brave man, Mr. Duane," she murmured, "the most courageous man I've ever known. God bless you, and good luck."

"Thank you. I'll need both."

The Ranger went out with Jeff Kelly, mounted Bullet as Kelly hurried to saddle his horse. He waved to Kelly and turned Bullet toward Abby's home. He rode over a back trail and reached the house without being seen by anyone. When Duane came in through the back door, Abby ran to him and thrust herself into his arms.

"Oh, thank God!" she cried. "I heard about it. I thought you had been killed. I was frantic."

She clutched him tighter, with a fierceness beyond her strength as if she wanted to mold herself to him, murmured against his chest. He suddenly felt a great affection for her wash through him. She was fine, decent, honest, and more than anything else she needed him, desperately. He realized that now with an overpowering sense of dismay. What, he wondered, could he say to her that wouldn't completely demoralize her at this moment when despair had turned to a great flooding of joy at his return.

There was the possibility, too, that he might die before the guns of Slap or Tulsa. He took hold of her arms and pushed her gently away from him, looked down into her face. He saw a great yearning for something intangible in her candid brown eyes. Her eyes always spoke her thoughts. They never hid anything.

She had been soft and yielding against him, eager, still a little frightened but the pleasure of being in his arms was the strongest emotion. She had quivered several times when he held her. He had a new vision of her. Now she was a little taut as she looked up at him.

"Abby," he said softly, "you have to face facts. I'm going to meet one, or two, very likely two, experienced gunfighters in the next hour. I think I understand how you feel about me. I wish you wouldn't. You may be hurt more an hour from now if you don't tell yourself there is nothing for us, for each other."

Abby dropped her hands and looked up at him through tears. She was dumbfounded, the intensity in her slim body conveying itself to him. The shock left her face but the paleness remained.

"Suppose," she said in a halting tone—"suppose it won't be that way? Suppose you—you win?" She half-turned from him, clasped her hands together and put them to her lips, biting the knuckles.

"Oh, God!" She turned back to him. "Help me, Buck," she pleaded. "Help me with the words." She was suddenly in his arms again. "I love you, Buck," she murmured emotionally. "I've loved you from the first day."

Buck Duane put his arms around her and held her close, bent his head and kissed her on the mouth, felt the salt of her tears against his lips. She was trembling again, and then she became a wild thing in his arms, her own arms clasped around his neck, her lips burning him with her frantic kisses. He tried to pull away from her but she held on. She held on desperately, the fear of losing him racing through her with a dizzying speed.

"Let me have my memory of love of you," she said then, and her shy woman's soul bent her head deeply into his chest. The words came muffled but unmistakable. "There's time. Let's have this hour."

It was no good. It would be no good for her and no good for him. The Ranger needed every emotion that possessed him now and in the next hour or two. His life depended on it. He tried to find the right words to say to her, the words that wouldn't leave her scorned, bring shame to her for having been refused, for what she was offering was the spirit and the life of her body and soul.

"If I could say what I would like to say, Abby," Duane said in the tenderest of tones, "I would tell you how much what you've said means at a time like this. Let's wait it out. Let's see what happens."

She stood there completely demolished in spirit for a long moment and then she turned away from him, but he reached out and took hold of her arm, pulled her to him.

"Not like that," he said softly. "Abby, things may work out. Let's hope for them. And say a prayer for me." He kissed her softly on the mouth. "Will you make some coffee? I have a few things to do. I'll be finished in about five minutes."

Abby seemed to recover herself and gave him a wan smile. "I'll hope," she said. "And I'll say a prayer."

The Texas Ranger went into his room, took off the belt that held his guns, got a piece of wax and a small bottle of oil and started to work the insides of both holsters, rubbing the wax and oil into the leather with the palm of his hand. He dropped a gun into the holster, pulled it out, then dropped it back. The action was smooth. He then examined both guns, cleaned them thoroughly, tested the trigger action. That, too, was perfect.

He put the belt back on, tied the holsters to his legs, moved them around in just the right positions for his draw. There was a grim look on Duane's face as he visualized what lay ahead. He heaved a heavy sigh and went into the kitchen. The coffee was on the table. He sat down and took a drink from the cup.

"Aren't you having any?" he asked.

"No. Not now. I have something to do." Abby turned swiftly, went into her room, closed the door, threw herself on the bed and gave way to the great sobbing that had threatened to burst forth all morning. Her body shook with her sobs as she lay there, her small hands clenched into fists, her face buried in the pillow to muffle the sound of her weeping.

She came out after a while, the ravages of her weeping erased from her face. Buck Duane was still at the table. She sat down opposite him.

"What will I do while you—you're gone?" she asked. "I just can't sit here and wait, and hope, and pray, and wait." Her tone was becoming desperate again.

"Would you rather come into town? Would you feel better if you were there, no matter how it came out?"

"Yes," she answered resolutely. "At least I'd know. There wouldn't be that terrible uncertainty, the torture of waiting to learn what happened."

Abby was in full control of herself, and he saw a new side of her. She had courage. She was willing to watch everything that mattered to her dissolve into nothingness with a single shot from a Colt.

"Are you sure you'll be all right?" Duane asked anxiously.

"I'll be all right," she answered firmly.

He rose. "You go into town now. Find Jeff and Sara Kelly. Stay with them. I think that will be better for you."

"Yes, I think it will." She stood up. "I'll go now."

Abby went into her room, picked up a shawl, threw it over her shoulders, came back into the kitchen, bent over him where he sat, and gave him a light kiss on the cheek. He stood up and smiled down at her.

"Don't miss," Abby said lightly. And then they both laughed and the tension dissolved. A deep surging of confidence went through him. It was all right. Everything was going to be all right. She went out the door without turning around.

Duane waited about ten minutes then walked into the rear yard, untied Bullet and mounted.

The center of town was crowded with people. Buggies, wagons, horses hitched to posts on both sides of the street met Buck Duane's gaze as he rode slowly in. His gaze probed the wooden walk outside the Osage. A group of men stood on either side of the batwings. The sun was high, the day bright. The Ranger looked up into the sky to note the slant of the rays. He wanted nothing to hinder him, not even a speck of dust an errant wind might throw up.

People stopped to stare after Duane as he rode past, whispered among themselves. Children pointed to him and shouted. Several small dogs barked at Bullet, who ignored them. He seemed to know that he was on an important mission and had no time to give to barking dogs. Duane rode up to the saloon, dismounted and ground-hitched Bullet. A man dashed into the saloon, and then another.

Duane waited patiently. He knew it was just a matter of a minute. He was right. Slap Wilson stalked out of the Osage and faced Duane. His facial muscles were corded, his face flaming with rage, his eyes gleaming with fury. His hands clenched and unclenched, and his voice was choked with passion as he spoke.

"You dirty night-crawling snake!" Slap Wilson yelled. His tone was hot and murderous, the hate burning through his words.

Duane gazed at him but did not answer. There was a glint of contempt in his eyes and his lips were in a straight, hard line. He said then, "I'm a Texas Ranger, Slap. You know that now. This is where you can settle your quarrel with me."

The crowd around the Osage scattered, the men taking placed against the buildings and the women huddling together in tight little groups. The street behind both men had miraculously cleared as Duane backed away, a step at a time, never taking his eyes off Slap Wilson.

Buck Duane knew one thing more than he knew anything else, that when you stepped out into the street to face the challenge of a gun you were more alone than if you suddenly had been violently thrown by some great force onto a strange and uninhabited planet. Survival now depended on your nerve, wits, speed of hand, keenness of sight, but above all, chain-lightning speed.

The wild anger in Slap Wilson diminished to some degree his judgment of time and distance, time measured in those cold and bitter instants that were like separate little eternities. Duane knew he had that much advantage.

As he backed away, Slap kept yelling at him, cursing him, spitting on the ground. "I'll kill you!" he cried. "I'll kill you! Kill you!"

Abby stood with Sara Kelly, their hands clasped together so tightly the blood had faded from the skin. Jeff Kelly stared at the scene before him, his eyes on Duane, who now was almost directly in front of him.

Abby Crowe turned her head for a brief moment and uttered a prayer. Sara Kelly whispered something to her and she turned her eyes back to the street. The whole tableau had a nightmare quality about it.

Duane stopped at a point in the street where the sun was just to his right and out of his eyes. There was not a rustle of wind, nor a sound from the crowd. All that was audible was a quick barking from a dog, and then it happened.

Slap Wilson cried out an oath. The depth of his hate could not go deeper, and it exploded into action. It was the moment Duane had waited for. He was sure that Slap would make that last oath and when he did he would reach for his gun. The sound of the oath had not yet died down when both men drew and fired. But Duane's gun had flashed a split second faster, so fast that few men saw the pull.

Slap's shot threw up dust a few feet in front of Duane, and then he stood there, stiff and erect, his head rolling a little from side to side, blood poured from his mouth, and he toppled forward. Abby let out a wild cry, started to run toward Duane, but Sara held her back.

"Don't!" she cried. "Not yet. Look!"

"Here comes Tulsa!" a man in the crowd yelled.

XIV

Abby Crowe turned into Sara Kelly's arms, unable to take more of the hot liquid tension that had piled up inside of her. Sara held her close, whispered words of encouragement.

"He'll kill Buck," Abby moaned. "He's killed twenty men. Oh, my God, my God!"

Jeff Kelly went between the two women, put his arms around them and spoke in a low tone. His words seemed to buoy up Abby's spirits as she turned her eyes to the road again.

The crowd remained stilled and the mischievous little dog that had barked was now held in the arms of a little boy who stood on the wooded walk staring fascinated at Buck Duane. He had seen something he had heard his elders talking about but never had believed it would come to pass before his eyes. Now there was going to be another time, in the next few minutes.

Duane had holstered his gun and stood there in the street watching Tulsa Harrow approach. There was a slight sneer on Tulsa's face as he walked up the street. He ignored the crowd completely. His eyes were fastened on Duane. He lifted a silver-handled Colt from its highly polished holster, inspected it briefly, spun the cylinder, dropped the gun back into the holster, then pulled it half way out and back several times to test the smoothness of the draw.

Satisfied, Harrow smiled a quick smile and looked directly at Buck Duane. He had moved just a few feet from where Slap Wilson lay dead, directly in front of the body.

"A Ranger, eh, Duane?" Tulsa sneered. "A damned

Texas Ranger. I might have known. Well, Ranger, this is where I wanted to meet you. Right here in front of all your goody-goodies. You've done a pretty good job. Got all my men killed and killed Slap. You're goin' to try me now, Duane. You know what? I'm goin' to see your guts spilled right where you stand."

Duane said nothing, just kept his eyes focused on Tulsa's right hand and his right foot, keeping them both in full view. He knew from things his father had taught him, that a gunfighter will make an untoward move with some part of his body just before he reached for his gun. The nervous movement might be made with the opposite foot, shoulder, or hand, but when he was ready to pull it would be made with the gun side.

Duane remembered that when he had talked to Kelly that day outside the courtroom he had made a movement with his left foot. If what his father had taught him held true then Tulsa would make the movement with his right foot.

Tulsa stood erect, his hands at his sides, his eyes holding Duane, watching him intently, those steely eyes never wavering for a moment. The hush that had fallen over the crowd was like the silence of death itself. It seemed that nature, too, had been stunned into silence for not a leaf rustled, a speck of dusk moved, nor even the mildest gust of wind drifted over the stretch of ground where both men stood.

Absolute silence had taken over as the crowd watched first one man and then the other. Abby stood there next to Jeff Kelly with her lips moving in prayer.

A man coughed just outside the door of the Osage. It seemed to be the signal for Duane and Tulsa to draw. Duane's eyes had kept Tulsa's right foot and right arm in constant view, his eyes glued to both members. When the man coughed, Tulsa's right foot moved imperceptibly, and Duane drew. If his draw against Slap Wilson had been fast then this one belied belief.

Both guns exploded at once, Duane's shot threw Tulsa violently backward and his gun fell from his hand and clattered into the dusty street. Tulsa's body and the shot from his gun seemed to coordinate in action for he fell at the split second that his gun went off. That was the speed of Duane's draw and the firing of his Colt.

Abby burst from between Jeff and Sara Kelly and ran sobbing toward Duane. The crowd began to mill around the two bodies and to stare at the fallen men. A doctor emerged from the crowd and bent over Tulsa.

"Through the heart," he declared. "Never knew what hit him." He looked toward Duane. "Never saw such shooting in my life for sure. That man is the fastest gun alive."

The crowd began to mill around Duane who held the sobbing Abby in his arms. She was weeping hysterically now, the deep relief at the outcome overwhelming her. Duane patted her shoulder and whispered to her soothingly. Sara Kelly came up and Duane motioned to her to take Abby and comfort her, help her to regain her composure.

Sara Kelly took Abby's arm and pulled her gently away. "Come on, dear. It's all over. There's nothing more to worry about."

Abby allowed herself to be led away, but not too far. She wanted to stay as close to Duane as she could. Jeff Kelly talked to Duane.

"It isn't over yet, Buck," he said. "There's Jonathan Finley. What about him?"

As Kelly spoke, Jonathan Finley came into view, a Winchester in his hands, his gray hair gleaming in the sun, his tall figure striding determinedly toward the street where Buck Duane stood.

The Ranger stood where he was, his eyes fixed on Finley, on the Winchester, waiting for the first movement that would warn him of Finley's intent to shot.

"God!" Abby cried. "Jonathan Finley!" She turned into Sara Kelly's arms. "This is awful, awful! I can't take any more," she sobbed.

"All you people get out of the way!" Finley yelled. "I want that white-livered skunk Duane!"

84

"Finley," the Ranger yelled, "drop your gun! You're under arrest!"

"Arrest?" Finley shouted back. "You dirty, two-timing snake! Come and arrest me!" He stood there shaking with rage, his head moving up and down and from side to side, his mouth working as if he were chewing something he couldn't swallow.

The crowd had scattered out of direct range of the guns, moved to the wooden walks fronting the streets. And at that moment Cathy came running up the street.

"Uncle Jonathan! Don't!" she screamed. She was weeping wildly. "Uncle Jonathan! Uncle Jonathan! Don't shoot! Don't shoot!"

She reached his side and pulled at his arm. He jerked away from her.

"Get out of the way, Cathy!" he yelled at her. "I'm going to kill this snake!"

"Finley," Buck Duane yelled, "don't make me kill you! Let's talk this over. You've still got a chance."

"Talk?" Finley shouted. He laughed on a high, eerie note. "You did things up fine with your damned talk. Killed off all my men, you did! Now you want to arrest me! Put me in jail, eh? Or hang me! I'll give you talk!" he raised his rifle and snapped off a shot.

As he raised his rifle, Buck Duane dropped to the ground, rolled, was up on his feet, ran in a zigzag line to the safety of a doorway. He couldn't shoot back, not while Cathy stood next to her uncle. The crowd that had taken refuge on the side of the street where the Ranger had run now scattered to the opposite side.

Abby and Sara huddled together holding each other, both women whispered anguished prayers. The drama of the situation had caught the crowd up in its depths and a greater stillness than that which had pervaded them before hung over them.

"You sleazy lawman!" Finley yelled. "Come out into the street!" He leveled the Winchester and fired, the slug tearing splinters of wood from the building where Buck Duane had sheltered himself.

"Cathy," the Ranger yelled, "get out of the way!"

But Cathy refused to leave her uncle's side. She was still making an effort to tear the rifle from his hands. Finley turned toward her and pushed her violently aside. As he did so, Duane threw his hat out toward the street and the anxious and half-crazed Finley fired.

The Ranger took two quick steps from the doorway, leveled his gun and fired. The slug caught Finley in the left shoulder and the rifle fell from his hands.

Duane moved toward him, gun in hand. "Stand right there, Finley. Don't make a move. If you reach for that rifle I'll drop you!"

Cathy leaped to her feet and ran to her uncle's side, took him in her arms. He was bleeding profusely. There was no more fight in him. He was a beaten old man, shaken, wounded, in obvious shock, and tottering on his feet.

The Ranger reached down and picked up the rifle, motioned to the crowd. "Send out the doctor!"

The doctor emerged from the group a short distance away and hurried to the wounded man.

"Patch him up," Duane ordered. "He's under arrest."

Cathy looked up at Duane, a great sadness in her eyes, her lovely mouth trembling, great beads of tears rolling down her cheeks.

"Why did you do this to me?" she asked in a tremulous tone. "Why?"

"I'm sorry, Cathy," Duane replied softly. "Truly sorry. There was no other way, no other way."

"It was cruel. You—you made me believe—" She turned her head away unable to continue, and followed the doctor, holding on to her uncle's arm.

Buck Duane motioned to Jeff Kelly. "Go with them. You won't need a gun but take the rifle anyway. It will probably be some time before he'll be able to travel. By that time Captain MacNelly should be here with the Rangers.

Abby ran toward him. "Oh, Buck, it was terrible! I've never been so frightened in my life. I'm glad you didn't kill him. And that poor girl. I'm sorry for her."

"So am I. I'm convinced she didn't know of her uncle's doings. She tried to stop him from shooting at me. It's a shame, all around."

The crowd stared at the Ranger in fascination. They had seen a man with great courage stand up before two vaunted gunfighters and best them. They had seen him react valorously in the face of powerful rifle fire and succeeded again, a feeling of vague satisfaction in them that he hadn't killed the old man, even though many of them felt that Finley had deserved killing.

Abby said, "Can you come home now, Buck? You must be awfully tired." There was a pleading in her tone.

He looked into her eyes and saw a great tenderness there, and a promise of things she wanted so much for him to take.

"Not yet, Abby. I have a prisoner in the doctor's office. I have to wait to see how he comes out. Why don't you go on home. You must be tired too."

She sighed heavily. "No, I'll wait. I'd like us to go home together."

Some of the crowd began to leave. The undertaker of the town called for volunteers to help him remove the two bodies from the street. Several men picked up Slap Wilson and Tulsa Harrow and carried them into the undertaker's parlor.

A group of young boys gathered on the walk opposite where Buck Duane stood with Abby and stared at him in awe, whispering among themselves.

About twenty minutes later, Jeff Kelly and the doctor came out. Abby gripped Buck Duane's arm, certain of what the doctor would say.

"Mr. Duane," the doctor said, and shook his head, "too old. Shock. Jonathan Finley died a couple of minutes ago. Anything you want me to do?"

The Ranger shook his head. "No, there's nothing left to do. Where's Cathy?"

"With him," the doctor replied. "She won't leave him."

Duane nodded his head in understanding. "All right,

doctor. I guess that's all there is to it. See that she's all right, won't you? Do everything you can for her."

"I understand," the doctor replied. "I'll do my best." He paused a moment. "I'd like to ask a favor, Mr. Duane."

"Certainly."

"I'd like to shake your hand."

The Ranger held out his hand and the doctor shook it, and the understanding between the two men was all in the handshake.

Buck Duane turned then to Abby, and took her arm. "Let's go home," he said. He looked into her eyes, and all the tension flowed out of him as they walked slowly up the small town's dusty main street.

THE LURE
OF BURIED GOLD

I

Captain MacNelly, Commandant, Special Force, Texas Rangers, and his companion, Sergeant Buck Duane, lounged in two of the shabby rockers that lined the lobby of the Buckhorn Hotel, on the Plaza de Armas, San Antonio, overshadowed by the great twin-spired cathedral.

"Figure you could locate a ton of looted gold, Buck?" MacNelly fired the question as casually as though he was asking for a cigarette.

He was a slightly-built, frail-looking man in his early thirties, possessed of a driving energy and stark courage that already had made him an outstanding figure in a frontier force whose exploits were the talk of the nation.

Duane's unsmiling pale blue eyes, set in flat-planed features, gave his face a somber cast. His blond hair, cropped short, showed white around the ears, and there was a taut wariness about him ingrained by years spent along the Border among desperadoes who usually had at least four dead men to their accounts. The notches on the ivory-butted .45 protruding from Duane's holster told their own sinister story, but Duane had never notched a gun in his life. That Colt was the legacy of his father, a veteran on the gunsmoke trail. Lead had finally cut him down, but he'd loosed his last two rounds with a bullet in his heart. Men called it muscular reaction, motivated by an ingrained urge to kill. The same dark passion lingered deep in Duane, although he fought to subdue it. In his hand that same gun had downed six, seven, eight men—he'd lost count, but every killing had been forced upon him, and had left its scar.

The Rangers wore no rigidly prescribed uniform. But the one Duane wore conformed enough to how a Ranger was supposed to look to make it unlikely that anyone would mistake him for a cowpuncher.

Texas Rangers packed a Winchester .44, Colt .45 and a sheathed knife. They fought like Indians, unencumbered by surplus equipment. A Mexican blanket, a small wallet in which were salt and ammunition, a little parched corn, and tobacco, and they were equipped for the field. Wild game provided food, when that failed a horse had sometimes to be sacrificed.

If Duane felt any surprise at his Captain's unexpected question, he showed none.

"You really believe there's that much gold in Texas?" he drawled, half humorously.

"I'm damned sure of it," returned MacNelly, with a touch of grimness. "That gold, one hundred and fourteen ingots, worth over three-quarters of a million dollars, was en route from the Consolidated Mining Company, Hillsboro, New Mexico, by wagon—Texas gold, consigned to the State Treasury in Austin. It was highjacked north of Hertzburg, Camino County, Texas. The four guards were killed, and only a teamster survived to tell the story. He died later, from wounds. That was a year ago."

"A year!" exclaimed Duane.

"The hold-up was played down," said MacNelly. "With an election coming up, the governor figured it would cost votes. He set the State Police, Pinkerton's, a slug of deputies, onto the trail. To date they've turned up nothing, beyond the abandoned wagon."

"So when the trail peters out they call in the Rangers," said Duane dryly.

The Captain shrugged. "You know how many men we can muster—two companies, not half enough to handle the Border gangs, which is our job. I guess the Governor figured it was out of our bailiwick. But now he's dumped it right in our lap!"

Duane rolled a smoke. "Any ideas?" he asked.

"Just one," said MacNelly. "My gamble is that the gold's cached. They found the wagon abandoned in the Aridos Hills. The county sheriff moved fast to block trails and waterholes. That gold weighed close to two-thirds of a ton, too much to slip through the cordon. I'd say those ingots are buried somewhere within a day's ride from the holdup spot. They'll stay buried until a chance offers to smuggle 'em across the Border."

"And our job is to locate 'em first?"

"Not our job," corrected MacNelly gently. "*Your* job. I kind of hate to load this on you, Buck, so soon after that business in Tafton."

Duane nodded grimly, remembering his desperate masquerade as a member of Jonathan Finley's gang of robbers in the Border area. Finley, a respected rancher, had been suspected by the Rangers as the ringleader of the outlaw gang, but no proof could be obtained. Duane had gotten himself taken on as a gunhand, witnessed an abortive bank robbery, and finally had killed Finley's ace gunslinger. He had managed to wing the maddened Finley when the rancher opened fire on him; but the outlaw leader had died of his wounds soon after.

"It didn't leave a good taste in my mouth," Duane said slowly. "Maybe this will be better. Gold-hunting's a more friendly thing than man-killing, any way you look at it."

Buck Duane sat chewing his cigarette and gazing out through the open doorway of The Buckhorn Hotel. The Plaza de Armas was a maelstrom of men and vehicles—trains of unwieldy carratas, solid wooden wheels shrieking on ungreased axles; huge Pittsburgh freighters grinding over the ruts behind long strings of plodding mules; dust-grayed prairie schooners hauled by weary oxen; jouncing yellow stages swaying on leather springs. Men swarmed there thicker than maggots on a carcass, dozens of men—straw-hatted mestizos, bronzed punchers, frock-coated gamblers, sober-clad traders—crowding the plankwalks, blackening the Plaza, bunched around cockfights, swirling in and out of saloons.

A lusty, riproaring city, Duane thought, crossroads of the Southwest, queen of the southern plains. Colorful, crazy, capricious. Then he became aware that MacNelly was waiting for his answer.

"Sure," he said. "I'll take a stab at it—my own way."

"Which is?"

Duane raised his shoulders. "If the gold's cached, someone's keeping cases on it. Maybe I'll just mosey up into Camino County and poke around."

MacNelly's eyebrows lifted. "Wearing those stripes! Dammit Buck, you'll stand out like a piebald in a dun herd."

"Labeled Ranger!" Duane's sober features creased into a grin. It took half a dozen years off his apparent age. "No —as a saddlebum. I'll buy myself some denims, rub them in the dust to make them look trail-stained, chuck these stripes and I reckon I'll pass."

"Don't forget to wind a loose-knotted bandana around your neck," MacNelly said, grinning back at him.

II

Buck Duane was loading his gear on his horse when the distant reports punched into his ears—three shots, two so closely welded that they seemed almost to blend as one, then a third. Following which, brooding quiet again enveloped the dreary spread of hills, their rounded summits yellowed by the early morning sunlight.

Somebody out at dawn to bag a little fresh meat, was his first thought, as he remembered a deer sign. But that, he decided, tightening a loop around the roll, just didn't make sense. The first two shots had the whipcrack quality of a Winchester; the third a deeper note, like the boom of a shotgun. Even in throwing lead at a herd of deer, who would manipulate a Winchester and a shotgun at almost the same instant? Clearly two hunters had been responsible for those shots. But why would one tote a rifle and the other a shotgun? A shotgun for deer! That didn't make sense either.

Vaguely bothered, Duane adjusted the roped roll behind the cantle of his leggy horse, as trailworn as himself. Bullet was a proud-looking horse ordinarily, but Duane had taken pains to give him the aspect of a dust-caked mount such as a saddlebum would have to settle for.

Still pondering on the three shots that had disturbed the serenity of a new day, he set a boot in the stirrup, swung into leather and raised the reins. At his customary jogtrot, Bullet proceeded down canyon.

This was wild, arid country and Buck Duane had no more than a vague idea as to his location. All he knew was that he'd ridden through a vast spread of sunblasted terrain and had made dry camp the previous sundown in what he had believed to be the Aristos Hills. From the appearance of the country, he'd figured there wasn't another human being within miles—until he'd heard those shots.

The sun had risen higher above the distant blue-shadowed mountains and the air began to hold a promise of furnace heat ahead as horse and rider wound between boulders that littered the canyon floor, between which squatty greasewood and thorny mesquite clung tenaciously to life.

Gradually the canyon walls dropped away and the pony jogged across a high bench, clothed with stunted growth, and grayed with alkali dust. Through a break in the hills, a wide valley, now washed by sunlight, came into view, spread like a map before the rider, a vast dun stretch of the country, spiderwebbed with the green of chaparral. Duane drew rein and sat inhaling the fragrance of a lazy breeze, laden with sage scent, and eying the vista.

So distinct through the crystal-clear air as to seem almost within rifle shot—though he judged it to be at least five miles distant—a ranch spread out below him, its rock-and-adobe buildings surrounded by a screen of tall cottonwood. Duane's eyes took in the long, one-story ranchhouse, bunkhouse, barns and corrals. The blades of a tall windmill spun steadily, flashing as the sun struck them. Ponies moved antlike around a wire-fenced pasture.

Dotted here and there over the great shallow bowl were other ranches. But the Ranger's gaze followed the course of a creek that meandered down the valley like a thread of silver and focused on the batch of buildings, rendered toy-like by distance, which clustered on its bank and were still partly veiled by the clinging mists of dawn. That must be Hertzburg, located on Dead Horse Creek, he reflected.

Bullet's ears pricked up. Harsh on the breeze came the bawling of a mule. Very likely it was owned by whoever had been out shooting at sun-up. Duane kneed his mount into motion, angling across the bench in the direction of the bawling, bent on satisfying his curiosity as to the nature of the game that needed to be hunted with both rifle and shotgun.

The ground began to slant downward. Rock-etched slopes rose in either side and Duane found himself traversing a gulch, thick-grown with chaparral, the branches of which whipped his head and shoulders as Bullet breasted through.

The pony broke out of the brush and the Ranger eyed a cabin, set upon a patch of partly cleared ground. It was low-built, sturdily constructed of peeled logs, clinked with mud, with a flat roof from which sprouted a verdant growth of grass and weeds.

The windows were glazed with sheets of transparent *veso*, or gypsum, Mexican style. The plank door, on raw-hide hinges, gaped open. From a small shanty barn adjoining a pole corral, a shaggy mule, head outstretched, extended raucous greeting. There was no other sign of life about the place.

Duane walked Bullet across the clearing, drew rein when he was within hailing distance of the cabin and yelled, "Hello, anyone there? Hello—"

The mule continued its braying. Beyond that, Duane's

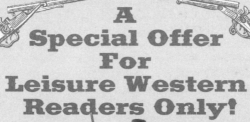

GET YOUR 4
FREE* BOOKS NOW—
A VALUE OF BETWEEN
$17 AND $20

Mail the Free* Books Certificate Today!

FREE* BOOKS
CERTIFICATE!

YES! I want to subscribe to the Leisure Western Book Club. Please send me my 4 FREE* BOOKS. Then, each month, I'll receive the four newest Leisure Western Selections to preview for 10 days. If I decide to keep them, I will pay the Special Member's Only discounted price of just $3.36 each, a total of $13.44 ($16.35 in Canada). This saves me between $3 and $6 off the bookstore price. There are no shipping, handling or other charges.* There is no minimum number of books I must buy and I may cancel the program at any time. In any case, the 4 FREE* BOOKS are mine to keep—at a value of between $17 and $20!

*In Canada, add $7.50 US shipping and handling per order for first shipment. For all subsequent shipments to Canada the cost of membership in the Book Club is $16.35 US plus $7.50 US shipping and handling per order. All payments must be made in US dollars.

Name _____

Address _____

City_____ State_____

Zip_____ Telephone_____

Signature_____

Biggest Savings Offer!

For those of you who would like to pay us in advance by check or credit card—we've got an even bigger savings in mind. Interested? Check here. ☐

If under 18, parent or guardian must sign. Terms, prices and conditions subject to change. Subscription subject to acceptance. Leisure Books reserves the right to reject any order or cancel any subscription.

Get Four Books Totally FREE* — A Value of between $16 and $20

Tear here and mail your FREE* book card today!

PLEASE RUSH
MY FOUR FREE*
BOOKS TO ME
RIGHT AWAY!

LeisureWestern Book Club
P.O. Box 6613
Edison, NJ 08818-6613

AFFIX
STAMP
HERE

shout was ignored. He lifted his reins, and rode closer. There seemed to be something ominous about the open door, the silent cabin, and the braying mule.

Suddenly, he stiffened. Midway between himself and the cabin, the windlass of a bricked well protruded above low brush. By the well, a lean-framed man was sprawled, face downward, his hooked fingers dug into the earth as though in agony.

Appalled, Duane darted another quick glance in the direction of the apparently deserted cabin, kneed Bullet and rode toward the prone form. Dismounting quickly, he paused for another swift look around, then turned the body over onto its back. Dark eyes, wide open, stared sightlessly up at him.

The dead man was clad in gray shirt and shabby overalls. Thinning iron-gray hair straggled over his ears, and his features were dour and deeply lined. A stubble of beard sprouted from his lantern jaw, and even the in death his rat-trap mouth was clamped shut. Close by, lying where it had slipped out of slackened fingers, lay a stubby double-barrelled ten-gauge shotgun. But what took Duane's eye were two puckered holes, crusted with dry blood, where the death-dealing slugs had punched into the hairy chest.

III

The mule had stopped braying. Silence enveloped the gulch like a shroud as Buck Duane stood staring down at the slain man. Almost automatically he reached for the shotgun, and ejected two shell cases. One was spent. That, he mused, would account for the shotgun blast he'd heard at dawn. And the two holes in the victim's chest tallied with the two rifle shots. Clearly someone had been hunting a man, not deer.

Lips pursed, he considered the killing. There were no powder burns on the dead man's shirt, no scorching, which had to mean the killing had not been close up. From the position of the body, the victim had apparently stepped out of the cabin and had been moving toward the well when he had been cut down. Apparently, also, he had been braced for trouble, or why would he have packed the shotgun. The odds were that some sound or challenge had pulled him outside.

Duane turned, eying the terrain beyond the well. It had been partly cleared of brush, but several thick clumps of mesquite still botched the ground, the nearest twenty paces distant. He moved toward it, and circled the clump, searching the sandy earth for some telltale sign. Quickly, he struck pay dirt—scuffed imprints of riding boots impressed on the loose soil, the sharp heels plainly defined.

The sunlight glinted on a brass shell case, nestling in a tuft of grass. He bent and picked it up, holding it on his palm for a moment while he studied it.

A picture took shape in his mind now—the killer crouched behind the thick-branching mesquite, a yell that had made the slain man pick up a rifle and dash from the cabin. The bushwhacker had loosed two shots. Hard hit, the victim had blindly gotten off one shot in return, dropped—and died.

The motive for the killing? Unconsciously, Duane shrugged. An old feud maybe, or robbery. He dropped the two .44 shell cases into a pants pocket, and headed for the open door-way of the cabin. When he stepped across the threshold and peered around in the muted light his eyes widened with surprise. He had expected to find the customary crude, homemade furnishings of a squatter's shack, knocked together from discarded boxes and scrap lumber. But there was nothing homemade here. The furnishings were handsome and for the most part of solid oak.

A leather-upholstered rocker stood by the fireplace, a half-filled bottle of Bourbon and a glass on the hearth beside it. Two chairs with woven rawhide seats were drawn up to a center table.

But it was plain an intruder had been foraging around;

for books had been swept from the shelves of an oaken case, and lay scattered over the packed-earth floor.

Moving past the table, Duane opened a door in the rear and eyed a lean-to kitchen, with iron cook stove, a deal table and bench and pots and pans dangling from nails on the wall. Nothing appeared to have been touched here.

But in the boxlike bedroom adjoining the living room, everything was in wild disorder.

The drawers of the bureau had been yanked out and its contents—shirts, towels, underclothes—strewn across the room. The top of a trunk that had apparently been locked had been pried off, and more clothing, sheets, books, papers, littered the floor, scooped out by fiercely impatient hands.

Surveying the wreckage, Duane noted a tintype lying face down on the bureau top. He straightened the photograph mechanically, and his eyes quickened with interest when he saw that it portrayed the head and shoulders of a young girl. An extremely attractive girl, he realized, eyeing it with appreciation.

Her features were well-formed and crowned by smooth-plaited hair wound in thick coils around a proudly-poised head. The level gaze of her large, dark eyes, combined with a touch of austerity about her mouth, conveyed an impression of cool self-assurance. Across the back, in an angular feminine hand, was written in ink, *"To Uncle James with love—Mildred."*

Well, she certainly was an extremely pretty girl, Duane thought and carefully set the tintype back on the bureau.

Moving outside, he stood considering his next move. It seemed plain that the motive for the killing was robbery. The ransacked bureau and trunk furnished evidence of that. Maybe the dead man was a prospector and had struck it rich. The Border was infested with desperadoes who would murder a man for his horse, or even for his boots. Likely some of the same stripe lurked in these hills. Living alone, the slain man had been an easy target. Duane knew it was his duty, even in the role of saddlebum, to report the killing to the law.

He closed the cabin door and headed for the shanty barn. Inside, he found the usual oddments of saddlery, a bridle, hackamore, and lash ropes. A pack saddle and kiacks were dumped in one corner, a half-used bale of hay in another. He lifted down the hackamore and picked out a rawhide lash rope.

The sun was arcing upward now, its fiery rays blasting the slopes. He slipped the hackamore over the mule's big ears, led it out. Sweat-soaked, he wrestled the dead weight of the stiffening corpse across the mule and roped it into place. Mounting Bullet, he pulled away from the scene of death, leading the mule with its grisly burden.

Dropping down into the valley, the little cavalcade wound its way through waves of rounded hills; left the hills behind and plugged over rolling swales that flowed across the valley floor. Ahead, chapparal bordering the creek made a verdant thread of green and in the distance rocky peaks were sharp-etched against the blue sweep of the sky.

Suddenly two riders came into view, bobbing up and down the swales as they cantered toward him from the direction of the ranch. When they drew closer, Buck Duane noted with interest that one was a girl. He checked his horse when they drew rein a dozen paces ahead and sat their saddles, wordlessly eyeing him.

The man, he guessed, was a cowman—a square-built, desert-eroded individual with features as weathered and expressionless as gray granite. Bleakly, he eyed first Duane, then the bloodied form roped across the mule.

But it was the girl who held Duane's attention. Vivid as a scarlet cactus, he thought, and likely as prickly. She was garbed in denim trousers, and a yellow silk shirt, open at the neck. A steeple-topped sombrero sat on a rippling mass of raven-black hair that flowed loose down her back. Her oval features were a delicate shade of brown, the texture of the skin flawless. Her red lips were willful and she sat the saddle with an unconscious air of arrogance. If she was aware of Buck Duane's intent, admiring gaze, she gave no sign of it.

"Who in hell are you, mister?" The cowman's voice was harshly challenging.

In no haste, Duane made a smoke, stuck it between his lips, plucked a match from his hatband and scraped it across the saddle. When he'd lit the cigarette, he replied, "Buck Duane, late of San Antone. And who might you be?"

"Cal Carson. I rod the CCC. I'm interested in knowing why you're crossing my range with a dead man."

Duane nodded toward the ugly seared-looking hills to the west. "Picked him up outside his cabin, back there. I had to take him into town or just leave him lying where he fell for the buzzards. I couldn't see myself doing that. Could you?"

"Who shot him?"

Duane raised his shoulders. "Your guess is as good as mine. Some jasper punched two holes in his chest with a Winchester."

"You pack a Winchester!" put in the girl. There was a subtle mockery in her eyes.

He eyed the butt of the rifle protruding from his saddle boot and smiled. "Since you make a point of it, ma'am, so does your—pard."

She turned to the granite-faced man beside her and commented, with amusement, "Next he'll be accusing you of shooting the man, Dad."

"Have you any idea who he is?" persisted the cowman, ignoring her.

"Wouldn't know him from Adam," confessed Duane.

"That's Jim Murdoch. He hung out in Wildcat Gulch."

"Surly as a bear with a sore head," added the girl. "He had a habit of taking after strangers with a shotgun."

Duane considered this new angle. Maybe Murdoch had loosed a load of buckshot at an unexpected visitor and the trespasser had become enraged and plugged him. But no, he reflected, the first two reports he'd heard had been those of a Winchester. Then there was the ransacked cabin.

"Everything points to robbery," he said. "The cabin's torn apart."

Unblinking, the cowman absorbed this. "You didn't get a glimpse of the killer then?"

Duane shook his head.

"Too bad!" said Carson. He touched his mount with the rowel and wheeled away. As she raised her reins to follow him, the girl's disdainful glance flicked over Duane's trail-stained clothes and he could have sworn she sniffed as the pony whirled around.

Finishing his smoke, Duane slacked in the saddle, staring after the receding riders as they cantered away across the plain. The girl had a touch of Spanish blood, he decided, and was likely as fiery as a mustang. But that didn't mean she wasn't pretty enough to turn the heads of nine men out of ten. He crushed his butt against a pants leg and heeled Bullet into motion again.

IV

The sun was beginning to slant westward when the buckskin's hooves drummed on the loose planks of a bridge that crossed the creek. Following the parallel ruts of a wagon road, Buck Duane emerged on a broad sandy widening of the trail that comprised Hertzburg's one and only street. On each side sat squat rock-and-adobe structures, with square-faced fronts, separated by alleys and weedgrown lots.

As Bullet jogged over the ruts, Duane's glance passed over a rambling general store, SIEGLER'S EMPORIUM lettered across its facade; a plank-and-adobe two-story structure, with rockers set upon a gallery that extended above the plankwalk, and whose weathered sign proclaimed it to be THE CROSSING HOUSE—ROOMS—ONE DOLLAR.

Life moved sluggishly in the heat of approaching noon and flies droned through the dry air. Here and there, saddlehorses lazily switched tails at the hitch rails. In shaded alleys, straw-hatted Mexicans squatted, drowsing or sucking cornhusk cigarettes, while a scattering of townsmen drifted along the plankwalks.

Drifting up street, he sighted a lean-to shack, propped against the side of the big rock-and-adobe Emporium. Above its doorway, a paint-peeling sign carried the words —EDWARD WELCH, TOWN MARSHAL.

Duane reined to the rail, dismounted and tied his animals. Townsmen began to gather, attracted by the mule's grisly burden.

When Duane stepped inside the shack the first thing that met his eyes were yellowing "Wanted" posters plastering the rear wall. A small pot-bellied heating stove and two straightback chairs filled most of the space. Ticketed rifles and handguns were heaped on a wide side shelf and a scratched oak desk was set under the front, and only window, a square of barn sash.

At the desk sat a sturdily built man, dehydrated down to bone and muscle. His faded gray eyes were set in a hawk-featured face, and a sun-bleached moustache drooped over his thin, humorless lips. His hair was iron-gray and thinning. He wore dark pants and a blue shirt, and a tarnished Town Marshal badge was pinned to his loose-hanging vest.

"I brought in a dead man," said Duane, and dropped onto a chair.

The marshal glanced out through the window, took in the body roped to the mule, and the curious townsmen and Mexicans clustering around it. His gaze came back to Duane, "That's Jim Murdoch!"

"So I hear?" said the Ranger.

"Did you kill him?"

Duane tautened, "Would I have brought him in if I had? I stumbled over the corpse outside his cabin, back in the hills," he went on, when the marshal continued to stare at him steadily. Then, remembering that Welch was only a

103

town marshal, he added, "Maybe that's outside your jurisdiction?"

"Nope," rasped the other, "I'm deputized to handle anything within county limits." He dug the makin's from a pocket of his dangling vest. "Suppose you give me the lowdown. First, just who are you, mister?"

"Buck Duane, late of San Antone."

"Hold a job anyways around?"

Duane shook his head.

The marshal's faded eyes traveled over his visitor's worn denims, washed-out shirt, and cracked boots. "Saddle-bum?" he inquired abruptly.

"Let's just say tumbleweed," said Duane.

Welch grunted. Duane had a feeling he'd somehow gotten off to a bad start. The thought that suspicion for causing this Murdoch's death might fall on him had never entered his mind. Now he realized that he was a stranger, had no witnesses, no apparent proof he hadn't shot the man himself.

Carefully, he began to relate exactly how he had become involved. He wound up by describing the condition of the cabin and gave his opinion that the motive for the killing was robbery.

"What's more," Buck Duane concluded, "I picked these empties up about forty paces from the cabin behind a mesquite clump. There were tracks of riding boots, too." He fished out the two .44 shell cases and dropped them on the desk.

Throughout, Welch had listened in frowning silence, drawing on his smoke. He picked up the empty cases, weighing them on a leathery palm and eying them speculatively.

Again he looked out through the window and Duane knew he was focussing the butt of the rifle protruding from the boot strapped to the buckskin's saddle.

"So you pack a Winchester," he mused, "and you lack means of support. Murdoch was a surly old cuss. Who's to say you didn't brace him for a handout? He threatens you with his scattergun. You plug him, clean out the cabin, cache the loot and pack the body to town, figuring to run a blazer over the law." In sardonic challenge, his faded eyes probed Duane.

"All right, Marshal," Duane said. "I can prove my hands are clean."

"I'm waiting!" threw back Welch.

Fuming, Duane led the way outside, elbowed through the clutter of men eying Murdoch's limp remains. He lifted his rifle from its sheath, and walked down the alley beside the shack, dogged by the marshal.

They came out upon an open flat upon which outhouses were spaced like gaunt sentinels, amid a litter of boxes, barrels and bottles discarded by the stores that lined Main Street. Levering a cartridge into the breech, Duane slanted the rifle upward and squeezed the trigger. The sound of the report brought a surge of townsmen into the far end of the alley. Duane ejected the empty shell, gingerly picked up the hot metal case, and extended it to Welch.

"Check!" he said curtly.

Without speaking, the marshal compared its base with those of the two expended shells Duane had previously handed him. The indentation of the firing pin was practically in the center of the brass base. On the other two shells the pin had struck midway between center and rim.

The lawman looked up. "Guess that clears you," Welch admitted.

"That's sure a weight off my mind," said Duane stonily.

"Quite gritting your teeth," advised the marshal, the ghost of a grin flitting over his bleak features. "Now we got to figure out who did put the jasper's light out."

"We!" echoed Duane. "You rod the law around here, not me."

"Sure," agreed the marshal, "and I'm riding out at sun-up to give that cabin a once-over. You're a material witness, and you're riding, too." His tone hardened. "Stick around town!"

"What if I don't pack the price of a room?" protested Duane.

"I got a cell you can use," said Welch dryly.

The Texas Ranger shrugged, realizing the futility of protest. "See you at sun-up," he said over his shoulder.

Duane headed toward the livery, walked his mount over the loose planks of the barn and dismounted at an empty stall. No one seemed to be around. He guessed the liveryman had sauntered down the street to inspect the mortal remains of Jim Murdoch. Stripping off his horse's gear, he spread the damp saddle blanket and led Bullet to water.

Then Duane dipped a double measure of grain from a bin, dumped it into the feed box and, while the horse munched, worked on its coat with currycomb and brush. The dusty-flank look would come back quickly enough after a good grooming. Tied to town by the marshal's edict, he had little to do and plenty of time in which to do it.

If he hadn't poked his nose into something which was none of his business, he reflected with disgust, he'd be free to proceed with his mission.

Outside, the shadows lengthened and an emptiness beneath his belt reminded him that he hadn't eaten since sun-up. He stepped back to admire Bullet's coat, now smooth and shining. Satisfied, he dropped the brush into a box and hit for the street.

Drifting along the darkened plankwalk, Duane brushed aside a musty fly curtain that draped the doorway of the restaurant, The Ritz, slapped his hat on a peg and slid onto a stool at the counter.

Thirty minutes later, feeling well content, a thick steak with all the trimmin's beneath his belt, the Ranger stepped outside. Yellow light from the oil lamps of the saloon opposite washed over ponies tied at the rail, and the narrow windows of the hotel made bright oblongs against the night.

Silhouetted against the steamy window of the hash-house, Duane paused to make a smoke and decide whether to drop into the saloon, The Bull Pen, or head back to the livery and spread his soogans on the straw pile.

Flame lanced suddenly from the black mouth of an alley beside the saloon. He felt the breath of a bullet that droned past his cheek, heard the sharp snick as it perforated the window behind him. Duane spun around in startled surprise and eyed a neat circular hole drilled through the glass, surrounded by a spiderweb of cracks. The roar of the explosion was ringing in his ears when he realized that, but for Lady Luck, that slug would have scattered his brains.

Again the gun spilled flame and thunder. More glass splintered. Duane jumped for the hitch-rail, ducked under it and zigzagged across the hoof-pocked street, jerking his .45 as he dodged over the ruts.

V

Buck Duane was aware of men spilling out of the saloon, attracted by the sound of the shooting, as he dove into the dark canyon of the alley from which fire had spurted. Toward the far end, he glimpsed the vague outline of a moving form and loosed a shot. A gun thundered in return. The slug, deflected by a rock-and-adobe wall, hurtled past in screaming richochet.

Crouching, Duane raced in pursuit, reached the end of the alley and paused, his lungs heaving, his eyes searching the night. To his right rose a stack of empty cases piled in the rear of the saloon, and ahead lay a trash-littered lot. To the left bulked deserted loading platforms and the square rear ends of stores.

Nothing moved. The would-be bushwhacker, he reflected, had had ample time to make a getaway. He could have ducked up another alley and by now was probably mingling with other citizens on Main Street. But the thought that someone was gunning for him wasn't comforting. The Ranger dropped the ivory-butted .45 back into leather and began to retrace his footsteps.

When Buck Duane reached the mouth of the alley he found it blocked with milling, shouting men. Across the street more were gathered, around the shattered window of The Ritz. Welch came up at a run, buckling on his gunbelt. "What's the trouble?" he demanded, thrusting through the throng.

"Some bushwhacking bastard took a couple of shots at me and hotfooted down this alley," Duane told him. "Seems one of Murdoch's pards had the same notion you did. He must have figured I'd downed the maverick and aimed to even things up."

"Murdoch never had no pards," said the marshal. "The old coot was as popular as a skunk at a picnic. Could be," he added thoughtfully, "that was Murdoch's killer, figuring you could read his brand." His tone sharpened, "Maybe he figured right."

"All I know about that killer is that he left two .44 shell cases behind," said Duane forcefully.

"Seems he got different ideas," said Welch. "Well, see you at sun-up."

"Don't gamble on it," said Duane, with wry emphasis.

The marshal chuckled dryly and slapped him on the shoulder. "If you're born to be hanged, you sure won't be shot." Welch either had a peculiar sense of humor, or was intimating obliquely that he wasn't altogether convinced of his innocence. Duane turned away with a shrug and headed for the livery.

A stable lamp, turned low, hooked onto an upright, spread a sicky aura of light in the big barn. From the gloomy recesses came the stomp of a restless horse, the rattle of a halter rope. Duane picked up his spooled roll and hastened toward the straw pile, enveloped in darkness. The gloom was comforting with a would-be killer on the loose. As he yanked off his boots, he damned a certain braying mule for the dozenth time.

The growing light of a new day stained the horizon crimson and Duane was polishing off the last of a stack of flap-jacks in the hash house when Welch jingled in. The marshal paused only to swallow a mug of coffee. Duane hastily cleaned up his plate and followed the lawman outside.

Shadows were still thick under the canopies of the plank-walks and the town slept, except for a grizzled old Mexican topping off the water barrels set along store fronts from a huge cask mounted on two creaking wheels and hauled by a bony mule.

The town marshal turned north when they crossed the plank bridge, following a trail that clung to the cutbanks of the sandy creek. It was pleasant riding in the freshness of early morning. Cottonwoods and willows made an um-brella of cool greenery; a squirrel scampered along a branch; cottontails bobbed through the brush; a coyote slunk across the plain with a stealthy backward glance. To make talk, Duane inquired, "This Murdoch been around long?"

"Most a year."

"Prospector?"

Welch eased in the saddle, brought out tobacco and papers. "Hell, no," he said. "The hombre's a retired mine superintendent from Hillsboro. His ticker went bad on him and he quit."

Duane remembered the girl of the tintype. "Any relatives around?"

The marshal yawned, and scratched a match. "He never said. But then, Murdoch always did keep his mouth cinched as tight as a miser's purse."

"Kind of fancied his own company?"

"That's right!" agreed the lawman emphatically. "The old moseyhorn wanted no truck with no one. He rode that doggoned mule into town every Saturday regular, picked up his chuck at Siegler's, ducked into The Bull Pen for two bottles of Kentucky Dew, and beat it back to the hills again. The old wart hog acted as sullen as a sore-headed dog. Once he ran some hunters off his place with a shotgun; and all they wanted was a dip of water from his ola."

Duane and Welch left the coolness of the shadowed creek and began angling across the flats toward the chaos of spiny hills and broken arroyos that lay to the west, already simmering beneath the searing rays of the rising sun.

"Carson, the CCC boss, braced me when I was bringing the corpse in," said Buck Duane.

"Another tarantula—so tough he has practically grown horns and is haired over."

"Which sure don't apply to his daughter."

"Part Mex. Pretty as a painted wagon, prickly as a procupine," agreed Welch. After which talk died between them.

When they dismounted outside Murdoch's cabin nothing seemed changed. A flock of plumed quail, dusting in the sand around the well, whirled away; and magpies chattered from the roof of the barn. As they walked toward the cabin door, Duane checked suddenly, gazing at the ground.

"There's been digging since I left," he announced abruptly, and pointed to freshly turned earth.

"You dead sure?" inquired Welch, squinting at the loose, sandy soil.

"Stake my saddle on it," Duane said. His glance traveled over the surrounding ground, patched with weeds and rank grass. "There's more! Some hombre's been gophering around."

They moved from one filled-in excavation to another, each about two feet square, its outline plain to the eye.

"Murdoch had something someone craved bad enough to kill him," Duane said. "Couldn't be it didn't come to light in the cabin so the killer skipped back after I left and got busy with a shovel."

"Any idea as to what it might be?" inquired Welch off-hand.

"Your guess is as good as mine," Duane said. "You claim Murdoch was a mining man. Could be he was prospecting on the side, located another Eldorado and squirreled up a slew of gold nuggets."

"Not in the Aridos Hills," declared the marshal emphatically. "They been raked over, never yielded an ounce of gold. Let's take a look at the cabin."

Welch stepped up to the door, levered it open and paused, eying the interior. Then he moved inside, bent and picked up two of the books scattered over the floor.

"*Chemical Minerology* and *Metalliferous Ores,*" he read aloud. "Murdoch spent too much time just reading," he growled and threw them aside.

They looked over the bedroom and the leanto kitchen, then returned to the living room. The marshal dropped down into the leather upholstered rocker, reached for the half-empty bottle of Bourton set on the hearth, took a long pull and passed it to Duane.

"I will say," he said, smacking his lips, "Murdoch had an educated taste—this is choice liquor."

Idly, Buck Duane stirred the litter of books on the floor with a boot. A fat envelope slid out of one. He picked it up, tossed it to Welch. "Maybe," he said, "that's the answer."

Marshal Welch slid a wad of greenbacks from the envelope, tallied them with blunt fingers. Three hundred and sixty dollars," he announced.

Instantly Duane was on his knees, shaking out other books, but nothing more came to light. "What do you make of it?" he asked, coming to his feet.

"Take your pick," said Welch, and reached for the bottle. "Robbery, or an old feud."

"Maybe the girl can help us."

"Girl?"

Duane stepped into the bedroom, returned with the tintype. The lawman squinted at it. "Never knew she existed."

"Could be there are letters around," said Duane.

Together, they sifted through the contents of the bureau and the brassbound trunk in the bedroom. But not a letter, or a scrap of written material came to light.

"Maybe Ma Purdy could help," said Welch, dusting off his pants knees.

"Just who is Ma Purdy?" Duane asked.

The deputy's black features creased into a grin. "A widow woman with a prying disposition," he said. "She's postmistress of Hertzburg. What Ma don't know about other folks business isn't worth the knowing. I gamble she reads every postcard that goes through the mail. I wouldn't even put it beyond her to steam open a letter occasionally —if it looked interesting. Come, let's go back to town."

It was midday when they reached town. A tinkling bell signalized their entry into Siegler's Emporium. The Emporium, considered Duane, glancing around, seemed to stock almost everything a man could desire. Merchandise-laden shelves lined the walls and showcases packed with cheap jewelry, knives, watches, and patent medicines crowded the floor. Foodstuff spilled out of boxes and barrels; rakes, hoes, buckets were suspended from the rafters. A pleasant aroma of cinnamon and ground coffee permeated the air.

A skinny woman, in a plain black dress, sorted mail behind a wicket in the rear, over which a sign carried the words, *United States Post Office*.

At their approach, her head jerked up and her eyes, bright and beady as a sparrow's, focused on Welch's weathered features. "So you been out to Murdoch's place. I reckon you're the first who ever got near the door without a buckshot greeting."

Even her chirpy tone was birdlike, and flat as a raven's squawk. Her glance darted from one to the other. "Well, what treasure was he guarding?"

"You're barking up the wrong tree, Ma," the marshal said shortly. "There's no treasure. Murdoch just craved to be left alone."

"To do what!" she sniffed. "Swill rotgut? Fiddlesticks! Why was he scared of peekers? He never even invited that good-looking niece of his in Tucson to visit him."

"Now just what would you know about that niece, Ma?" inquired Welch persuasively.

"She teaches school and she has great expectations," replied Mrs. Purdy.

"Expectations of what?"

The widow raised thin shoulders. "When he wrote the girl at Christmas—" she cut off abruptly, compressing her thin lips.

The marshal glanced meaningfully at Duane. "Well?" he prompted.

"Well," said Mrs. Purdy, "it's my impression he left her plenty."

"There are nothing but rocks and rattlesnakes in Wildcat Gulch."

"That's what you think," snapped Ma. "Maybe Si Leeson, the lawyer, knows different. He made up Murdoch's will."

"Guess we'll drop in on Si," decided Welch. "I'm sure thanking you, Ma. I'm thinking we've got a real smart postmistress."

"Happy to oblige, Frosty," she said, looking flattered, "although you know how I hate to pry into other folks' business."

VI

There was nothing that he liked, Buck Duane decided, about Silas Leeson, attorney-at law. The room that Leeson used as his office, off the lobby of The Crossing House, was little larger than an oversized closet. When Duane entered at the heels of the marshal he saw a corpulent individual, garbed in a seedy Prince Albert coat and baggy striped pants. His soiled white shirt was brought together at the neck by a faded silk cravat and the buttons of a brocaded vest were loosened to accommodate the contour of a bulging belly.

Duane was reminded of an overripe melon going to seed —an impression that was enhanced by the lawyer's pudgy features and a bulbous nose etched red with tiny broken veins.

The small office was already crowded by the ancient roll-top desk at which the lawyer's form lumped, a bookcase packed with musty yellow tomes and two straightback chairs.

At their entry, Leeson abruptly thrust a bottle into a desk drawer and became busy shuffling papers.

"Good day to you, gentlemen!" he said. Despite physical decay, the lawyer's tone still held a certain depth and resonance. "I assume your visit pertains to the corpus delecti."

"You guessed right!" Welch dropped into a chair, and lifted tobacco and papers from a vest pocket. "I hear Murdoch made a will."

"And entrusted it to the keeping of his legal advisor, to wit, myself," boomed Leeson.

"He have anything to leave, beyond that cabin and quarter-section?"

The lawyer laced fat fingers across the swell of his paunch. "A client's communications to his lawyer are as sacred as those of a patient to a medical practitioner," he said smugly.

"Quite going legal on me," barked Welch. "I've got a murder on my hands and I'm hunting motive. What did Murdoch own that would justify a killing?"

Duane could have sworn that amusement, maybe derision, sparked in Leeson's watery eyes. "Nothing," he returned smoothly, "beyond said quarter-section and the appurtenances thereto."

"Who's heir?"

"A niece. She resides in Tucson and her profession is that of school teacher."

His forehead furrowed, the marshal busied himself making a cigarette.

"You will have an opportunity to interrogate the lady later," said Leeson. "I have already sent a telegraphic message from the depot to Tucson. She should arrive in ample time for the funeral."

"There'll be an inquest, too," said Welch and rose. "Well, I guess we'll hold our hosses."

Outside, Duane commented, "Leeson didn't help any. All wind and bombast."

The marshal spat. "Si's as slick as a greased hog. He had a big reputation, back east, before he hit the booze." He shrugged, "Well, maybe we'll get a lead from the girl."

Railway service on the branch line that terminated at Hertzburg was confined to a mixed passenger-freight twice weekly. At ten in the morning, two days later, Duane hunkered against the clapboards of the squat little depot, watching the distant black smoke that plumed across the flats. The girl was entitled to some sort of a reception committee, he reflected, even if it consisted of only one man. Welch was busy rounding up jurors for the inquest.

Through an open window behind him came the intermittent clatter of a telegraph key.

Ten minutes later, with a hiss of steam, the big-funneled engine rolled into the station, its bell tolling solemnly. Coupled behind it were a wood-headed tender, solitary passenger coach, two box cars, express car and caboose.

Duane came to his feet as passengers began spilling from the coach—a robust ranch wife, two drummers, and a waspy little man in a shiny serge suit. Finally—a slender-waisted girl in her early twenties. That tintype sure hadn't lied, Duane told himself.

With a confident stride, a carpet bag swinging from one hand, and a big purse looped on the other, the girl moved toward the depot. She wore a severely-cut black bodice, fastened high in the neck with a plain silver brooch, while the hem of a dark skirt brushed the tops of her high-button shoes. A neat bonnet was set upon a mass of auburn hair and her eyes—green as jade—hinted at cool self-possession.

Duane stepped out to intercept her. "Miss Stokes?" he inquired, removing his hat.

The girl stopped walking and her green eyes appraised him. "Who are you?" she inquired.

"The name's Duane—Buck Duane. I was the one who found your uncle's body." He reached and relieved her of her carpet bag. "Guess you need to freshen up. It's only a short distance to the hotel."

"Have the caught the man who killed Uncle?" she asked, dropping into step beside him.

Duane shook his head. "They will," he said.

Too quickly for his liking, they reached the hotel. Miss Stokes registered and retrieved her carpet bag. She flashed a brief smile. "Thanks so much for your help," she said and swung away.

Somewhat taken aback by so abrupt a dismissal, Duane headed for the inquest.

His testimony was soon over, and the verdict was, predictably, "Murder by person or persons unknown."

"What next?" Duane asked the marshal.

"Have you seen the girl around?"

"Sure, she's at the hotel."

"We may as well have a talk with her—right now."

They found Mildred Stokes seated in one of the well-worn leather rockers that lined the hotel lobby, listening—with obvious distaste—to Silas H. Leeson, who sat lumped in an adjoining rocker.

At their appearance, the lawyer rose, bowed ponderously to the girl and told Welch in sonorous tones, "I have informed this charming young lady as to the nature of her legacy and expressed the opinion that, since there is so little possibility of its being contested, I can see no reason why she shouldn't enjoy the full use of the property forthwith."

Leeson waddled away. Welch dropped into his vacated rocker and Duane sank down on the other side of the girl.

Mildred Stokes stared with displeasure at the rotund lawyer's receding back. "That man has been drinking," she announced forcefully. "He positively reeks of liquor. Furthermore, I don't trust him."

"Do you have any reason for mistrusting him ma'am, apart from that?" inquired Welch.

"I certainly have. I am the sole surviving relative. Uncle Jim gave me to understand that when he passed on I would be a wealthy woman—that I would never have to work again. This—alcoholic—insists that the estate consists merely of a scrubby quarter-section of land, practically worthless, with a small cabin attached to it." Her voice quivered with indignation.

"I'm afraid he's right," Duane pointed out. "I'd say the land wouldn't bring a dollar an acre. The cabin—" He raised his shoulders. "A hundred dollars, at most."

The girl stared at him tight-lipped, her green eyes flaming with anger.

"What gave you the idea the property was valuable?" Welch asked.

"His letters. He used such phrases as 'Fortune has rewarded me to an unbelievable extent' and 'I am now a wealthy man and this wealth will be yours.'" She paused an instant, then went on with cold exasperation, "This Leeson person insists there is not one dollar in real money. He claims I am actually liable for the expense of interment, *his* fees, and certain other legal charges." She laughed without humor. "On a school teacher's salary!"

Welch brought a wad of currency out of a back pocket. "Maybe this will help," he said. "Over three hundred dollars in greenbacks. Duane found the money in the cabin, hidden in a book."

Miss Mildred Stokes took the bills in grim silence, and thrust them into her purse. "Thank you!" she said.

"You'd better keep the find to yourself," cautioned the marshal. "Leeson will otherwise claim it's part of the estate. Once his grubhooks fasten on greenbacks you can usually kiss them goodbye."

"You can depend upon me, Marshal Welch," she assured him composedly. "Well, I suppose I better prepare for the funeral." She smiled quickly, rose and headed for the stairway.

"It's kind of curious, Murdoch peddling that kind of talk," murmured Welch, building a smoke.

"You forgot the digging?" said Duane.

117

From the moment when he'd stumbled on Murdoch's body just the fact that the slain man lived near the town where he'd gone to see if he could pry some vital information out of Welch had stirred a vague puzzlement in his mind. How many dark secrets did the town hold, and did such killings occur often there?

Could it possibly have some remote connection with the looted gold? But now, in view of what he had since heard, and the fact that Murdoch had been a newcomer to the region his puzzlement had sharply increased, and suspicion had taken a firmer hold on his mind.

VII

The marshal came to his feet. "That digging has me buffaloed," he admitted. "Well, I guess there's no point in hobbling you. You are free to leave town—any time you want to go back to saddlebumming again."

"That's mighty comforting," drawled Duane.

The Texas Ranger considered his next move. It was clear to him that he had better get busy on the job that had brought him to Hertzburg—locating close to a ton of looted gold. Curious he should stumble over a possibly related mystery. The murdered recluse had promised his niece wealth, and had apparently left her nothing but a barren quarter-section. And why the digging? And the shot that had been aimed at him in town? Wasn't that plain proof that someone, likely the killer, had reason to believe that there was more than rock and scrub on Murdoch's holding?

Captain MacNelly would say it was no skin off his nose. Duane had an important assignment and local crime was the business of the county sheriff.

A bland-featured man, balding and draped in a rusty frock coat, slid quietly into the lobby. He had the long, acquisitive nose and guileless eyes of the born trader, and

118

his lips were as tight-locked as a rattrap.

The newcomer sank into a rocker and sat with an air of patient resignation, nursing a plug hat on his lap.

The Ranger drifted across to the desk. "Who's the frock-coated hombre?" he inquired.

"Mr. Siegler," the clerk tol him, low-voiced. "Owns the Emporium, this hotel, the saloon and most of what's left of the town," he went on. "Acts as undertaker and rents out the hearse. I gamble they don't plant their stiffs more handsome in San Antone than we do right here in Hertzburg."

In no amiable mood, Buck Duane entered The Ritz the next morning for breakfast. The shattered window of the hash house had been boarded up and the yellow light of a dangling oil lamp bathed the form of a solitary patron at the far end of the counter.

Duane slapped his hat on a peg and became aware, with a start, that the diner was Mildred Stokes. Well, he reflected, she hadn't shown any great desire for his company and he wasn't thrusting it upon her now. Sliding onto a stool as far distant from her as possible, he gave an order for flapjacks and coffee to the impassive Chinese behind the counter.

His head swiveled at the sound of her voice, tinged with amusement. "Did you really think, Mr. Duane, that I'd sell my uncle's place to you, or anyone else, for a mere pittance?"

"I wouldn't take it as a gift," he replied gruffly.

"Yet there are folks who would pay up to fifteen hundred dollars."

"Maybe they've been out in the sun too long," he countered.

She raised her shoulders. "They seem like hard-headed business men to me. One, a Mr. Carson, offered me a thousand cash. Another, who goes by the name of Connors, was willing to pay fifteen hundred, if I'd accept a down payment of five hundred."

"I'd say the gents are out of their minds," retorted

Duane, striving to strain the interest out of his voice. "The value just isn't there. They give any reasons?"

"Mr. Carson, a cowman, claims he wishes to demolish the cabin. He says it is likely to habor rustlers."

"Makes sense," admitted Duane, "but not a thousand dollars' worth."

"Mr. Connors raises horses. He plans to use the cabin as a hunting camp."

"A mighty expensive hunting camp!" Duane said derisively. It was plain, he thought, that he was not alone in believing that Murdoch had cached something worthwhile on that quarter. "There's something smells about both deals."

Mildred Stokes' green eyes appraised him calmly. "I think the smell, as you term it, emanates from a different source—from the direction of a drunken lawyer and—a few other people I could mention."

"You take a look at that quarter section, and you'll change your mind," Duane assured her. "I could take my pick of ten thousand acres out in the hills, homestead a quarter for two bits an acre and throw up a cabin for fifty dollars. Being a schoolma'am, you can figure out how small the outlay would come to."

"Those men are not fools!"

"Maybe they figure they're buying more than just land."

"What, for instance?" she demanded sharply.

"I just wouldn't know," he admitted slowly, spilling molasses on his flapjacks. He began to eat. The girl, pre-occupied, munched buttered home-made bread.

"I'd like to see Uncle's place for myself," she announced suddenly. "I can't leave Hertzburg for two days anyway."

"You ride?" he inquired, between mouthfuls.

"A little."

He glanced at her voluminous skirt. "In that?"

"I imagine the store stocks overalls."

"It would be a pleasure to take you out there," he said.

The sun was high when they left town. Miss Mildred Stokes straddled a hack rented from the livery. An oversize pair of bib overalls, stiff with newness, covered most of her, except the top of a white blouse. From the way she bumped leather and latched firmly onto the saddlehorn, Duane guessed her riding experience was strictly limited. But they jogged along the trail that followed the curves of Dead Horse Creek without mishap.

Before pulling away from the welcome shade of the chapparal that clothed the creek, he called a halt. Mildred Stokes dismounted stiffly, ruefully easing cramped limbs. "Is it much further?" she inquired.

The Ranger hated to tell her that they had scarcely started and the worst lay ahead—the long drag across glaring flats, and a tedious climb up into the hills.

"Not so far," he replied evasively, and busied himself slacking cinches and rocking saddles.

Flayed by the sun, wreathed by a halo of dust stirred up by the horses' hooves, the two dragged across the parched expanse of the valley floor, while the silhouettes of sullen hills ahead seemed to recede rather than to draw closer. There was no talk between them.

The girl, Duane guessed, was suffering torment, galled raw by the saddle. Her lips remained tight set, and she stared fixedly ahead from beneath the side brim of a felt hat. Whatever Mildred Stokes lacked, Duane thought, it wasn't spunk.

Shadows had begun to slant eastward when they rode into the clearing and halted by the shany barn. Miss Stokes slumped in the saddle, her eyes closed, obviously exhausted. Buck Duane lifted her down and packed her limp form into the shade of the barn. Heading for the cabin, he routed out a towel and a bucket, and hit for the well.

A great deal of hard toil had gone into the digging of that well, he reflected, dropping down the wooden bucket suspended by a rope from the windlass. It was square and a good three feet across, its top rimmed by a coping of adobe

121

bricks. Duane heard the bucket splash, and wound it up, slopping water.

Her body sagging against the warped clapboards of the barn, the girl wearily opened her eyes at his approach. Her white blouse was now a dirty gray, and the neat coils of her braided hair had loosened and straggled in disorder over her ears. But it was plain she was beyond fretting about her appearance.

Duane set the bucket of water beside her, and dropped the towel into her lap. "Dampen your face, and rest awhile," he said. Few women unaccustomed to the saddle, he knew, could have made that ride.

He looked around for more evidence of digging, and found plenty. It was as if a gopher had moved in—a human gopher. Some of the earth had been so freshly turned that the sound of their approach could have scared the digger off.

When Mildred Stokes hobbled stiffly around the angle of the cabin, he was still looking down at the pitted ground. Her hair was again arranged in neat coils and she had washed the grime from her face, and beaten the dust off her overalls.

She entered the cabin,

"Well, what do you think?" Duane inquired, when she reappeared.

The girl shrugged and said nothing.

"Now take a look around," he suggested, with a sweep of his arm.

She stood staring at the grim hills, etched with protruding rock and the scrubby brush. Then her gaze returned to the desolate cabin.

"What you figure the place is actually worth?" he asked.

"Ten cents!" she said and smiled tiredly. "I think I'll accept the thousand dollars Mr. Carson offered, before he changes his mind."

"The land isn't worth a third of that," he agreed. "It's what's hidden under it."

"I don't understand."

"There wasn't a spadeful of earth turned over when I found your uncle. Now look!" He indicated the numerous mounds of earth that specked the ground. "Someone's hunting something—and it's not just a mouldy saddle overgrown with weeds."

"You mean, you think Uncle buried his—his wealth?"

"Murdoch promised to leave you plenty. Why would he lie? Why was he shot? Why all this digging?"

"But I can't stay out in these desolate hills and guard the place," she protested. "I have to return to Tucson. I have to teach."

There was an almost pleading look in her green eyes. Duane fingered his chin. "I suppose," he said, "I could stick around, for a week or so."

And there'd be hell to pay, he thought, if Captain MacNelly ever thought I was letting myself in for helping out a lady tenderfoot—and neglecting my job!

VIII

Wearily, Mildred Stokes turned to the Ranger. "I really can't afford to pay for your time," she said, a look of defeat in her eyes.

Buck Duane raised his shoulders. "I'll donate the time," he assured her offhand. "There's chuck enough in the kitchen to feed me for a month."

"It's very kind of you," she said and her relieved smile was sufficient recompense.

"Forget it!" he returned gruffly. He eyed the sinking sun. "I guess we'd better hit the trail back to Hertzburg now."

She ran her hands down her buttocks with a wry grimace. "Couldn't we wait until it's—just a little cooler? I can't face that heat again."

Buck Duane agreed promptly. Mildred Stokes appeared

to be in a more amiable mood and the prospect of spending a few extra hours in her company was not displeasing to him. He carried out the upholstered rocker, set it in the shade of the porch and padded it with a blanket. With a sigh, the auburn haired girl sank gratefully into it.

The gulch was etched with shadow and the hills faded behind purpling veils when they pulled out. A sage-scented breeze whispered through the brush and brightening stars powdered the heavens. Dust fogged thick around them but, somehow, it didn't seem so bad.

When they jogged down the dim canyon of Hertzburg's Main Street the town was asleep and darkened, except in the vicinity of The Bull Pen and the lighted windows of the hotel. Outside The Crossing House they pulled to the rail. Mildred Stokes slid slackly out of leather and stood slumped against her mount, grasping the saddlehorn for support.

"You'd better let me help you inside," Duane said, eying her sympathetically.

"No!" she retorted, with a touch of spirit, and began limping across the plankwalk. Midway, she paused and turned. "Thank you—for everything, Buck," she said softly.

He raised a hand in farewell and reached for the dangling reins of her rented mount. Kneeing the buckskin, he hit for the livery.

There was no sign of Mildred Stokes when he downed breakfast in The Ritz the following morning. With hope that she'd appear, he hung around the hotel lobby until midmorning, then decided that she'd be likely to spend the day in bed, recuperating from the ride.

While he was loitering in town, he reflected, odds were that the unknown digger was gophering back in the hills. She was banking on him to protect her interests. His place was at the cabin. With no great enthusiasm, he rigged Bullet and pulled out.

In no haste, he was jogging across the flats when the thud of fast-moving hooves on the sun-baked ground brought his head around. Wreathed in dust, a buckboard whirled toward him, hauled by two half-broken broncs. There was no mistaking the driver. Dark hair streaming, sombrero bumping her back, was Carson's dark-eyed daughter, Rosita.

When the rig drew abreast, she hauled the sweat-plastered broncs to a halt. Duane, spitting dust, eyed her irately.

"Do you have to run the bejabbers out of those horses?" he demanded.

"How I handle my team is none of your business," she flared. "You misplaced your whey-faced school-ma'am?"

"Maybe you should stop nosing into my business," he said.

"Like inquiring if you two had a good time in the cabin last night?" taunted the girl.

"We were not at the cabin."

Rosita's long, unbound hair rippled as she tossed her head. "Stop spilling windies," she threw back. "I watched you two heading for the hills through dad's spyglass. You never rode back."

"Since you've got eyes like a cat, you should know better," he threw back with amusement.

"You calling me a cat?" she flamed.

Some impish impulse led Duane to prod this fiery girl further. He gravely eyed the hot color that tinged her cheeks, and the resentful twist of her red lips. His flat-planed features creased into a grin. "I'd say you were a ringtailed bobcat, fit for nothing but clawing."

In a spurt of temper, she swung at him wildly with the lash of her braided quirt, dangling by its loop from her right wrist. The leather thong whistled through the air. He ducked, an arm instinctively raised to protect his face, and she swung again.

The lash struck his forearm, coiled around it like an angry serpent—and bit like a red-hot branding iron. He kicked free of the oxbow stirrups, slid off his horse and grabbed the taut thong with his free hand. He hauled. The loop biting into her wrist, Rosita fought to retrieve her quirt. Duane reached, grasped her extended arm, and yanked her off the seat of the buckboard.

Rosita teetered, lost balance, and dropped into his arms, her legs flailing and fingers clawing. A furious panting bundle of feminity, she fought to break free as he grabbed her, striving to curb her clawing fingers without using undue force. Sharp nails raked his neck and his temper rose.

He spun her around, jerked the quirt free of her wrist and flung it aside. Then he crooked a knee and held her, writhing, across it. The flat of his right hand descended upon the taut seat of her jeans, again and again.

"Maybe a sound walloping will teach you to think twice before you use a quirt on me again."

Finally, he set Rosita down on her feet. Her breast rising and falling, she stood glaring at him. Her eyes were blazing cauldrons.

"You beast!" she choked. "If I had a shotgun, I'd shoot you dead."

"You're not to be trusted with a peashooter, much less a gun," he said.

"I hate you!"

"Too bad!" he said. "Now head back home before I beat some more dust out of the seat of your pants."

"You wouldn't dare!"

With the ghost of a grin, Duane moved toward her. She hastily spun around, scrambled up onto the seat of the buckboard and grabbed the lines. The restive broncs took off with a rush, scattering dust.

Duane stood watching the rig bounce away over the swales. Miss Rosita Carson, he decided, fingering his lacerated neck, was a regular spitfire. He was about to mount when he glimpsed her quirt lying in the dust. Picking it up, he looped it on the saddlehorn.

Nothing seemed changed when he dismounted at Murdoch's place near the pole corral. Quail still dusted themselves beyond the well, and the magpies, handsome with their white markings, skittered around the cabin roof. He stripped the gear off Bullet, watered the animal and loosed it in the corral. Smiling faintly, he eyed Rosita's quirt, then hung it from a nail in the barn.

Next he gave attention to the cabin. Here a clean-up job seemed in order. He gathered up the volumes scattering over the living room floor and slid back onto the shelves of the oak bookcase. After which he started restoring a semblance of order to the bedroom, replacing the contents of the bureau drawers.

A folded newspaper lay on the bottom of the lowest drawer. He saw that it was a copy of *The Hillsboro Herald* and the date showed it to be over a year old. Curious, he opened it up. Just why, he wondered, would James Murdoch have treasured a year-old newspaper?

The pages crackled with dryness as he idly rifled through them. Suddenly, his attention quickened. One news item was roughly circled with a pencil mark. It was headed: OUTLAWS LOOT GOLD SHIPMENT. With growing interest, he read:

Four guards were killed and a teamster wounded when a shipment of gold ingots from the Consolidated Mining Company, valued at over $750,000, was held up on the Logan Grade, about ten miles north of Hertzburg, Texas. The ingots were en route to Austin, Texas.

According to James Mullen, the wounded teamster, at least four men were involved in the outrage. Mullen states that the wagon carrying the gold was laboring up the rocky grade when there was a sudden burst of gunfire. A slug struck him in the neck, knocking him to the ground. Despite pain from the wound, he lay motionless, playing dead, and saw four masked men ride up to the wagon.

One dismounted, climbed up to the driving seat, picked up the lines and drove away, while his pards dropped in behind. The whole affair was over in minutes and had obviously been carefully planned.

It was not until late afternoon, seven hours later, that a prospector, heading into town for supplies, came across the bullet-riddled corpses of the guards and the wounded teamster, who was delirious with pain. Before nightfall, the teamster recovered sufficiently to gasp out the story of the holdup.

At time of publication, no trace of either the looted ingots or the renegades has been found, although posses are scouring the country.

Jack Curtis, manager of Consolidated, states that no effort will be spared to recover the gold and bring the outlaws to justice. In order to foil such holdups, he said, shipments were made at irregular intervals and the dates of departure were known only to office personnel. Because of this and the fact that a gold shipment has never before run into trouble, four armed guards were deemed sufficient.

Conscious of rising excitement, Buck Duane stared at the yellowing sheet. Was this the key to Murdoch's murder and the mysterious digging in the vicinity of the cabin? Town Marshal Welch had said that the dead man had been superintendent of the Little Sheba Mine, at Hillsboro, New Mexico, who had "retired" and had been living in the cabin for about a year. Could he have been a member of the gang, keeping cases on the cached gold? Were the looted ingots lying somewhere around, buried until an opportunity arose to move them down into Mexico? Could the wealth Murdoch had promised his niece be his share of the loot?

There must have been a reason for Murdoch's bushwhacking, the search of the cabin, the digging. The sensible thing to do would be to head into Hertzburg and hash it over with Welch. He had put off doing that too long.

IX

The town marshal looked up when Buck Duane jingled into his office. "What brings you back? Figured you'd shed the dust of Camino County."

The Ranger ignored the question. "What you know about this?" he asked, and plunked the aging copy of *The Hillsboro Herald*, in front of the lawman, indicating the penciled item.

Welch scanned the account of the hold-up silently, looked up. "How did you come to latch onto this?" he wanted to know.

Duane scraped up a chair, dropped into it and told of his deal with the schoolma'am to keep an eye on her property and his discovery of the news sheet when he was straightening up the cabin. He checked an impulse, which he had controlled from to first, to reveal his identity to Welch. Maybe he'd get further, he thought, if he stuck to his role of saddlebum.

"That looted shipment ever recovered?" he inquired.

Welch shook his head.

"Could be it's cached," Duane said. "Right there on Murdoch's quarter-section."

"Just what put that notion into your head?" The marshal asked, eying the Ranger with amusement.

"The sign points that way. Murdoch quit his job in Hillsboro near the time of the holdup. He locates within a short day's ride of the scene. He promises his niece he'll leave her well-fixed. He's bushwhacked and some hombre starts digging. What more do you need?"

"Plenty," threw back Welch and fingered for the makin's. "You seem to be weaving a whole blanket out of one oddment of wool. Murdoch was clean as a hound's tooth. Likely, some loco prospector got a notion the old carrion crow was wallowing in velvet. He beefs the hombre, searches the cabin, but overlooks the wad you located. You bull in and scare him off. He ducks back whenever chance offers and digs like crazy, hugging the idea he'll turn up aces. I'd say it's as simple as that."

"Could be," agreed Duane doubtfully. "How far did the law get clearing up the case?"

"No further than you could throw a posthole," admitted the marshal placidly.

"Why was that?"

Welch, a deliberate man, touched a match to his smoke. "Not one clue," he said, "outside the abandoned wagon, found in the hills beyond the grade. I scoured the Aridos with a posse. Sheriff Harrigan, down at Cochrane, threw in a slew of deputies. I'm pretty sure every waterhole and trail from here to the Border was watched. Consolidated even brung in Pinkertons. When the dust settled, all we'd come up with was that abandoned wagon."

"You figure the gold was cached?"

"Nope!" returned the marshal promptly. "I figure it was halfway to the Border before the sheriff started spreading his dragnet. Them ingots weigh twenty-seven pounds apiece. A mule could pack six—more at a pinch. A twenty-mule train could handle a ton and a half of gold—and move fast. Hombres smart enough to pull off that hold-up would be slick enough to plan their getaway."

"Just supposing the ingots were cached. Why not Murdoch's place?" persisted Duane.

"Why Murdoch's?" retorted Welch with patient resignation. "Ain't there ten thousand other likely spots? Why drag Murdoch in? Hell, he was a big shot in Hillsboro, superintendent of the Little Sheba Mine for most ten years. What's more, he was a sick man—his ticker was acting up. He'd just got back from a long spell in some eastern hospital. He warn't even around when the gang hit. He was taking it easy back in the hills.

"And, if he was tied in with the renegades there'd be no call for them to dig all over creation. They'd know just where they'd planted the loot, and exactly where to dig." He snorted. "I'd stake my saddle that gold crossed the Border less than twenty-four hours after it was lifted."

Duane sat rubbing his chin, considering this. "You're wrong, Welch," he said finally. "My gamble is that the gold's lying out at Murdoch's place right now. Here's the way I've got it figured. Murdoch's health forced him to quit. He was flat broke, on account of the high-priced eastern doctoring.

"So he planned the robbery. He picks up the hideaway in the hills, spreads it around he's retiring. Being on the inside, he knows when big shipments go out. He hunts up three, four hardcases and lays out the holdup plan. It goes off like clockwork. The ingots are cached on his place and the gang sits back to wait—until the searching posses cool off."

"The hardcases get impatient, shoot Murdoch—and

then forget where they planted the ingots!'' put in the marshal, amusement flickering in his faded eyes.

The Ranger shook his head. ''Murdoch keeps cases on the cache. I've an idea he was real shrewd that way. He begins to ask himself why he should split with three or four gun dummies. He'd figured everything. He was the brains and they were just tools. He's living alone, with time to kill. All he has to do is move the ingots to another spot, and tell the dummies to go plumb to hell. But he outsmarts himself. They get sore, kill him, and comb the cabin for a clue as to where he's moved the loot. Finding none, they start digging. Now,'' he challenged, with a faint smile. ''Pick that to pieces!''

''A gent with your arguing talent is wasting time drifting saddle-loose around the country,'' declared Welch gravely. ''You'd make a mint as a range lawyer.''

''I doubt that,'' smiled Duane. ''It seems you're not convinced.''

''Not enough to plow up Murdoch's hundred and sixty acres,'' commented the marshal dryly.

When Duane left the law shack he paused on the plank-walk, fashioning a smoke and mentally debating whether or not to acquaint Mildred Stokes with his theory about the looted ingots. Probably she wouldn't take kindly to the thought that her uncle had been involved in the theft of a gold shipment. But his discovery of that newspaper had changed his whole set-up. If his idea held water, the week he had proposed to spend out at the cabin would be wasted time.

Murdoch's tough sidekicks would simply outwait him, then jump in when he rode off and dig at leisure. He had to stick around until his theory was proved or disproved. Miss Stokes was debating selling to Carson or this horse raiser. He had to persuade her to hold on.

When he arrived at the hotel, the sun was low in the sky and Main Street was bisected by long banners of slowly reddening radiance.

Mildred Stokes was slumped on one of the shabby rockers in the lobby of The Crossing House, plainly still suffering from the effects of her ride, and plainly bored by the attentions of a florid-face drummer.

A look of relief came into her eyes when she saw the Texan. She rose quickly and moved across the faded carpet toward him.

"You appear to be a mite saddlesore," commented Duane. "It happens to everyone at times."

"A mite!" she repeated wryly. "I have a feeling I'll never sit down in comfort again."

"It will pass," Duane assured her and steered her to a nearby seat. "Read this!" he said. He pulled out the creased copy of *The Hillsboro Herald* and passed it to her, indicating the marked account of the hold-up.

"Well?" she inquired, when she had read it slowly and carefully.

"I've got a crazy notion that gold may be buried on your quarter-section."

The young teacher's eyes opened wide with surprise. "Whatever gave you that idea?" she exclaimed.

He hesitated. "It's never been proved. But there are some ugly rumors floating about that your uncle was tied in with that robbery."

Her smooth forehead furrowed. "You make me more curious than ever," she said. She did not appear to be as shocked—or outraged—by what he had said as he had feared she might be.

"Well, this is how I figure it." Again, he outlined his theory concerning the holdup, and her uncle's possible part in it. To his further surprise, she heard him out without protest.

When he was through, she said thoughtfully, "Mother always believed that the Murdochs were never overly scrupulous. It seems she may have been right. So that's why those men were so anxious to buy!"

"I'm far from convinced of that," Duane told her. "Carson could have had a half-dozen reasons for wanting it. I hear the CCC's plagued with rustlers and that cabin could serve as a base for their operations. As for Conners, possibly he figured Murdoch chased visitors away because there was something he'd discovered about the property he didn't want anyone to know about. Something that made it valuable, perhaps, but not necessarily hidden gold.''

''Well,'' she demanded, with a touch of irritation, ''what action do you suggest I take?''

''Let me stick around, and see if I can locate the gold. Maybe I've been tilting at windmills. With luck, we could pocket a hundred fifty thousand dollars in bounty money for finding those ingots.''

''That large a sum!'' she breathed. ''It seems incrdible!''

''Seventy-five thousand apiece.''

Her green eyes questioned him sharply.

''A fifty-fifty split,'' he said. As a Ranger, he knew that he could not share in the reward—but it would be out of character for a ''tumbleweed'' not to insist on sharing in it.

''Yes,'' she said slowly, ''I suppose that would be fair.''

Duane stood up. ''Since we seem to be in complete agreement I may as well head back to the hills.'' He smiled. ''I guess that gold has gotten under my skin. I mean, just the possibility that it may actually be there. I'd hate to leave the place wide open.''

When the jingle of his spur chains died, Mildred Stokes sat deep in thought, her small chin cradled on the palm of one hand. The drummer, lighting a fresh cigar, lumbered across the threadbare carpet to renew their acquaintance. Ignoring him, Mildred rose and headed for the street. The creased copy of *The Hillsboro Herald* lay on the floor beside her rocker where she had dropped it accidentally.

Town marshal Welch, deep sunk in thought, glanced up with surprise when the door opened and Mildred Stokes walked in. Hastily, he rose and pulled a chair forward.

She glanced at the hard wooden seat and repressed a shudder. ''I prefer to stand,'' she told him.

Welch chuckled. ''Saddle sores? Duane should have known a city girl can't bump leather for hours without raising blisters.'' He perched on a corner of the old oak desk. ''Well, ma'am, what's on your mind?''

''Duane has just been in to see me,'' she began, without preamble. ''It seems he's almost sure that stolen gold ingots, valued at perhaps three-quarters of a million dollars, are buried on the property my uncle left."

The marshal nodded, his faded eyes weighing her. "That's right," he said. "He was in here about an hour ago, trying to convince me."

"Do you believe he could *possibly* be right?"

"I'd say he's been smoking loco weed."

"Assuming the ingots did come to light," she asked, ignoring his comment, "your duty would be to take possession of them in the name of the law, wouldn't it?"

"I'm afraid so, ma'am," the marshall said.

"Isn't there a possibility that he might—decamp?"

"You mean run off with the gold?" Welch grinned. "Not a chance. It could weigh a ton and a half, supposing it's there—which I seriously doubt.

"You could be mistaken," she insisted. "Someone should keep a close watch on him. I'll be hundreds of miles away, in Tucson. My interests should be protected. I think that obligations devolves upon you."

"So you don't trust Duane?" he mused.

"I would trust anyone where three-quarters of a million in gold, or a hundred-fifty-thousand-dollar bounty, was involved," she retorted coolly.

X

When the Ranger jogged into the holding deep in the hills it was past midnight. A segment of moon laid a spectral sheen over bouldery slopes, while the discordant howling of a coyote pack floated across the barren ridges.

Duane stripped off Bullet's gear, turned the horse into the corral and headed for the cabin, packing his Winchester. Scarcely had he yanked off his boots in the boxy bedroom when the first shot shattered the brittle gypsum window pane, and buried itself in the timbered wall on the far side of the room.

Buck Duane dove for the kerosene lamp set on the bureau and doused the light. Ducking low, he moved quickly to the shattered window and peered out, his eyes level with the sill. Nothing moved. Wan moonlight washed over the dim outlines of hills and ridges; his horse made a lumpy blur in the corral and a startled bird fluttered through the night. A tiny tongue of flame licked through the obscurity.

Duane's head jerked down as the whipcrack of a second rifle shot reached his ears. He heard a thud as the bullet slapped into the timbers of the cabin. Groping, he found his Winchester and moved out into the living room. Here he hunkered by the fireplace, nursing the rifle, waiting and watching.

Lead continued to drone steadily into the timbered flank of the cabin. The marksman was apparently firing from a low ridge that paralleled the holding to the south, Duane told himself. It was long-range for a Winchester, which was probably why he couldn't find the window again, not without a light inside the shack to guide him. Just what did the coyote think he was gaining by random shooting?

It was difficult to resist the temptation to slip out and scout around. There had been four men in the hold-up gang, he reminded himself. They could all be lurking out in the night, ready to cut him down the instant he emerged. Thick log walls made the cabin practically bullet-proof. It would be smart to wait for dawn before poking around.

He began to nod. It had been a long and wearying day. Sleepily, he stretched out on the floor, the rifle beside him in case there was trouble.

In the early morn the squawking of magpies aroused him. He sat up, blinking drowsily around. Day had dawned. A broad shaft of sunlight speared through the window. Remembrance of the shooting flowed into his mind. He came quickly to his feet, stepped to the window and peered out.

It would have been hard to conceive of a more peaceful scene. The plumed quail were back, happily dusting beyond the well. Jewelled humming birds darted through the clear air and a sparrow hawk circled high overhead.

Opening the door, Duane slid outside, rifle slanted, brace for trouble. But nothing disturbed the serenity of the new day. Bullet stood hipshot in the corral, the quail arose with a whirl of wings, and the ridge from which a rifle had spat lead during the night lay bare and barren, bathed in early morning sunlight.

The Ranger packed a bucket of water from the well, started a fire in the sheetiron stove and filled the coffee pot. Waiting for the coffee to boil, he mulled over the shooting, and decided it could have but one object—to scare him off the place. If the rifleman had felt an urge to kill, he could have ghosted close and fired point-blank through a window. Duane made a mental note to drape those windows.

Even though his brain was well pickled in alcohol, Silas H. Leeson was possessed of considerable acumen and a complete lack of scruple. Despite this, he was perpetually in a state of financial insolvency. There was little legal business in Hertzburg and what there was came mainly from Julius Siegler. Siegler, a past master in the art of squeezing a dollar, considered that a room in The Crossing House, plus office space, amply compensated his legal aide for services rendered. This arrangement frequently left Silas short of funds to assuage a gnawing thirst.

He was in this aggravating condition when he wandered into the hotel lobby and plunked down into a rocker, running his tongue over dry lips. This was Saturday, the one day in the week when Hertzburg came alive. Ranchers, punchers, homesteaders from all over the valley headed for town, to meet and mingle, visit the stores and trade talk. The Bull Pen invariably did a land office business but Silas' credit had long run out.

Tortured by enticing visions of smooth Bourbon and jovial conviviality, the corpulent lawyer sat and suffered.

Incuriously, he picked up a newspaper lying on the floor beside the rocker, sighted an item outlined in pencil and became absorbed. Then inspiration dawned.

Julius Siegler was busy with his books in the rear of The Emporium when Leeson waddled down an aisle, a folded newspaper under one arm. At sight of the fleshy form bulking in the office doorway, Siegler growled, "No advances!" and continued figuring.

"Julius," remonstrated his visitor, "you totally miscomprehend the object of my visit."

"Never knew a time when you didn't need money," snapped the storekeeper. "What else could bring you here?"

Leeson chuckled with hearty goodwill. "At this time my financial affairs are of no consequence. What would you say if I offered to enrich you to the tune of some hundred thousand dollars?"

"I'd say you were drunk—as usual," grunted Siegler.

"You do me an injustice, a gross injustice," protested the pudgy lawyer. "Here, sir, is my proof!" He folded the newspaper to display the marked item, and tossed it on the storekeeper's desk.

Siegler sighed, pushed a ledger aside, picked up the yellowed sheet and perused it swiftly. "Well?" he demanded, looking up.

"Those looted ingots have never been recovered."

"Just what are you getting at?"

"At the present moment they're buried on a quarter-section bequeathed to a Miss Mildred Stokes. The bounty for their recovery, my dear sir, is one hundred and fifty thousand dollars."

"Murdoch's place!" Siegler pushed up his green eye-shade, leaned back in his chair, and laced bony fingers across a lean middle. He eyed the fleshy lawyer shrewdly. "So that's why there's been talk of digging up there," he murmured. Leeson noted, with elation, that the tone of his voice registered rising interest.

"The magnet's three-quarters of a million in ingots," asserted the lawyer. "With an absentee owner, interlopers have a free hand. This is a golden opportunity, Julius."

"To pack a spade up into the Aridos, chasing a will-o'-the-wisp?" The storekeeper's tone was dryly ironic.

"To acquire the property, run off trespassers and explore at leisure."

Siegler eyed his flabby legal adviser closely. "Just what gives you the notion that those ingots are cached on Murdoch's place?"

Leeson's slack features creased into a sly smile. "Certain significant statements made by James Murdoch at the time he made his will." He knew he was embroidering the truth, but who was to prove otherwise? Murdoch couldn't argue, he was dead. When he'd drawn the will, he'd been surprised when the recluse had listed only one rocky quarter-section as assets. Plainly, the crusty ex-mine superintendent had more.

A reasonable assumption was that he had converted his real assets into gold and what was more logical than to assume he'd buried the gold. It had been a happy inspiration to transform that presumably existing gold into looted ingots. Who would disprove the allegation?

"And just what were those significant statements?" inquired Siegler, with a frowning glance.

"Professional ethics forbid me to repeat them," said Leeson smugly. "I will say, under a seal of strict confidence, they indicated Murdoch was involved in the robbery."

Musing, Siegler eyed the paper. He looked up, his eyes as sharp as dagger points. "You're not giving me a run around, Si?"

"Why, Julius!" The lawyer's voice quivered in stricken protest.

"Just why haven't *you* grabbed these ingots—and the bounty?"

"They have yet to be located first," explained the lawyer patiently. "The right to search demands ownership. Could I afford to buy?"

Musing, the storekeeper abstracted a wooden toothpick from his vest pocket, and worried his front teeth. "Can the girl sell?" he demanded, abruptly.

"She can assign," said Leeson promptly. "Then, immediately probate proceedings are completed, the

138

assignee will assume title."

"*Would* she sell?"

"Give me one reason why a sensible woman would hang on to a worthless quarter-section," chuckled the lawyer. "Providing, of course, she was offered a satisfactory financial inducement."

"Get Miss Stokes' best cash price," snapped Siegler, "and move fast."

"Indeed I will, Julius," Leeson assured him quickly. "That will involve a trip to Tucson," he said smoothly. "Personal persuasion is imperative. A small advance—"

"How much?" demanded the storekeeper, frowning irately.

"A hundred dollars."

Siegler slid open a drawer of his desk, lifted out a metal cash book, and carefully counted out five gold eagles. "Fifty dollars!" he rasped. "Not a cent more."

"If you say so," agreed the lawyer, striving to cloak his exhilaration. Siegler counted the coins in his eager palm.

In high good humor, Silas H. Leeson pushed through the batwings of The Bull Pen. His strategem had worked. No longer were his pockets empty. He'd outslickered Siegler, and that old skinflint was as slick as a greased hog. Probably there wasn't a dollar buried on that barren quarter-section. But who was to prove it?

The five gold eagles burning his pants pocket were a mere trifle in comparison to the honorarium he would add to whatever price the girl set. Siegler would buy. He had no doubt of it. The old tightwad had swallowed the bait, even if forking over the gold eagles had stuck for a moment in his gullet.

The saloon was crowded. Punchers from the CCC, Diamond, Currycomb, Running W., and townsmen, occupied all of the tables, with a sprinkling of cattle buyers, drummers and itinerants. At one end of the bar, cowmen bunched, trading cattle talk. At the other, Town Marshal Welch nursed a bottle of beer. The air pulsed with the steady drone of men's voices, punctuated by the clink of glasses. Blue clouds of tobacco smoke eddied and swirled.

Clutching a full bottle of Bourbon in one hand and a glass in the other, Leeson found space at a table and settled down. Six drinks later he was telling himself he was undoubtedly the smartest man in Hertzburg, if not in the entire state of Texas. He deserved to be treated with dignity and respect, and not like a legal "has been" just one notch above a saddlebum. Well, he would impress upon these yammering clods that Silas Leeson was a man of stature, that his acute mind had solved a mystery that had baffled the town marshal, the sheriff, even Pinkerton's.

"Gentlemen!" His rich, round tones boomed above the rumble of talk. "I have an announcement to make."

Talk cut off abruptly. Heads swiveled and patrons focused on Leeson's inflamed features, and bleary eyes.

"He's as drunk as a fiddler's clerk," grinned a puncher seated nearby.

Leeson weaved to his feet, clutching the edge of the table for support. "You will be happy to learn," the lawyer said, staring around him, "that the location of certain gold ingots, to the value of three-quarters of a million dollars, plundered over a year ago, is now known to your humble servant, Silas H. Leeson." He attempted to bow, staggered, and almost fell.

"You don't say! Where's the gold cached?" inquired the puncher, dropping a wink around his table.

"That sir," replied the lawyer, with drunken gravity, "is a confidential matter that must remain locked up here." He solemnly tapped his forehead. "I will, however, drop a hint—a certain quarter-section is involved." That he was close to blind drunk was clearly evident, but that he was unaware of what a spectacle he was making of himself was just as apparent.

Well pleased by the attention he had attracted, Leeson tilted his bottle, sank down in his chair and most inelegantly flopped across the table, amid roars of laughter. Talk broke out again and Silas H. Leeson, Hertz-

burg's prize drunk, was forgotten. That didn't bother
Silas—he had sunk deep into booze-sodden slumber.

At dawn a swamper stumbled over Leeson's stiffening
form in the alley beside the saloon. The lawyer was not a
pretty sight. His skull had been smashed by repeated blows
inflicted by a heavy weapon. It could have been the barrel
of a Colt .45.

XI

Back in the hills, Buck Duane inched around the lonely
holding, debating on his next move, and uncomfortably
aware that he was a sitting duck for any lurking bushwhacker. There was little doubt in his mind now that the
looted ingots were cached somewhere on Murdoch's
quarter-section. The shooting of the previous night had
provided ample proof that at least one member of the
renegade gang was hanging around, resenting his presence
enough to open fire on the shack.

They had probably gambled that Murdoch's killing
would be laid to a feud, or a quarrel with some half-crazed
prospector, and the place abandoned, leaving them with a
free hand to search for the hidden gold. In their eyes he
was an unexpected obstacle—a wandering saddlebum who
had blundered blindly into their business. If they failed to
scare him off, what would their next move be?

An hour later Duane was back in town. Slacked in his
chair, the town marshal listened without comment when
Duane told of the rifle shots. "It should be plain to a blind
mule," the Ranger concluded, "that the hombre, or
hombres, who beefed Murdoch are hellbent to scare me
off. If you can come up with any good reason, outside of
those looted ingots, I wish you'd spell it out."

"Maybe you got it figured," agreed Welch, adding

another butt to the litter around the stove.

"So you've finally seen the light!" said Duane ironically.

"Si Leeson was picked up in the alley beside the saloon this morning," Welch told him.

"Drunk?"

"Dead—his skull busted."

Despite his startlement Duane found himself wondering why Welch had so abruptly switched the subject. "Leeson get tangled in a fracas?" he asked.

"Could be, but I doubt it."

In response to Duane's questioning glance, the lawman informed him of the lawyer's drunken announcement in The Bull Pen the previous night. "Si was liquored up," he ended. "Quite possibly someone thought he knew too much and talked too much."

"You mean—you think one of Murdoch's pards was listening in?"

"It's a strong possibility, I would say."

"Well, what more proof do you need?"

"Just a little more might help," Welch said. "But I'm beginning to see it your way. Everyone in and out of town was tanking up in the saloon last night," he went on glumly. "No one was anywhere near the alley." His eroded features creased into a humorless grin, "You got the brains of a canary bird, you'll go hightailing it out of town before you join Si in boothill."

"Guess I've got a streak of mule in me," said Duane. "I'm sticking."

"All right. I've no objection to having someone around I can talk to now and then—when bullets start hitting people in crazy ways. You have a few ideas about it, and that's more than can be said for just anybody."

Duane rode back to the hills in the heat of midday. To his surprise, two saddlehorses were tied to the rail of the corral. One glance told him they were Carson's dun and a bay mare the cowman's daughter straddled. He wondered wryly if Rosita's father had ridden out to demand an accounting for the spanking. His cogitations were interrupted by the appearance of the girl. Nonchalantly she strolled out of the barn, idly twitching her quirt.

"Are you accustomed to making yourself at home in other folks' premises?" he asked.

"Only when they're concealing stolen property," she retorted. She flicked the quirt, and stood looking at him with lofty disdain.

"I don't see that flat-chested schoolteacher around," she said mockingly. "Don't tell me you've been using my quirt to scare her away."

"Miss Stokes is a lady, and behaves like one." Duane's voice had a snap to it.

"And you are as blind as the bats we have to smoke out of the bunkhouses to be taken in by her," she flung back at him.

He fingered the healing scratches on his neck inflicted by her raking nails. "A man's hardly blind when he prefers a woman who doesn't claw like a wildcat."

"I should have clawed your eyes out!" the girl said.

"I knew you were fully capable of doing just that—or trying to," he informed her, stepping out of leather. "What brought you up here?"

"We heard shooting," Duane spun around at the sound of Carson's harsh accents. The stocky cowman had just rounded the angle of the barn, and had clearly caught a part of the angry exchange of insults. "My boys been riding nights, on account of brand-blotchers," added the rancher. "They reported hearing gunfire up here. Figured I'd better look into it."

Carson's voice hardened. "Guess you and me had better have a little talk."

"Any time!" Duane told him, and began stripping off Bullet's gear. "Someone loosed some shots at me last night. I haven't the least idea why."

The girl wandered away. Carson sank on his heels against the barn, watching Duane water his mount and loose it in the corral. The Ranger dropped down beside him, began building a smoke, and inquired, "What's on your mind?"

"You!" barked Carson. "Just why are you sticking around?"

"It could be I'm watching the place for Miss Stokes."

Carson eyed him narrowly. "What needs watching—the sagebrush?"

Duane said nothing.

"You wouldn't be tied in with the coyotes who are rustling me blind?"

"Ask Welch whether he thinks I'm a rustler or not," Duane said. "You'll get an answer that will make you drop that idea pronto."

"So you claim," rasped Carson. "If I thought this place was likely to become a rustlers' hideaway—I'd burn it to the ground."

"Maybe that's why I'm staying—to make sure nothing like that happens to Miss Stokes' property. Brace her if you want to buy."

"I already braced her," Carson said, "and drew a blank."

"How do you know she doesn't plan to settle here?"

The rancher snorted. "A schoolma'am—alone! You must be loco."

Duane shrugged. "Whatever she decides to do—it's none of my business."

"Listen," grunted Carson. "I'll pay you to make it your business." He pulled a roll of greenbacks from a back pocket, and peeled off five bills. "Stick this hundred dollars in your jeans, then hit for Tucson. Make her see the light and I'll add another hundred."

"Not interested!" said Duane shortly.

"Buck me and you'll get gored," bristled the rancher.

Duane came to his feet. "I'm sticking right here."

"I got other ideas," fumed Carson. He straightened and strode, stiff-legged, toward his saddlehorse.

Carson's daughter had been drifting around close by and Duane guessed that she hadn't missed much of the talk. Thumbs hooked in his gunbelt, he watched the infuriated rancher loose his pony and swing into the saddle. Indolently Rosito followed suit, trailing her father as he pulled out. When her bay passed Duane, she checked the animal and called out, "Stubborn as a steer!"

"I can prod, too," he threw back.

"But you can still be corraled!" she taunted, challenge flashing in her dark eyes. Before he could feel he had evened the score with a suitable reply she roweled the bay and cantered out of earshot.

He stood watching father and daughter as their mounts wound through brush and boulders down gulch. If it wasn't enough to have the mysterious marksman gunning for him, he now had Carson on his neck.

When he turned and started back toward the cabin, he saw that the door was ajar. So Carson's daughter, and maybe her father, had gone inside. He had no sooner passed through the door and stepped into the bedroom then he came to an abrupt halt, quick anger sparkling in his eyes. The tintype of Mildred Stokes lay on the floor, the sheet of glass behind which it was framed, ground into small fragments. It could have been crushed by a small heel.

XII

As the setting sun reddened the upthrust peaks of the distant mountains, sending long, duncolored shadows wavering across the clearing Buck Duane's thoughts reverted to the shooting of the previous night. Would the unseen marksman be back with darkness, plonking lead at the cabin again?

When the hills finally faded behind thickening veils of purple, he draped the windows. Then he lit the lamp and prepared supper. By the time he'd cleaned up a mess of fried beans and bacon, darkness clothed the gulch. He slipped outside into a dim shadowland.

Picking his path carefully through the obscurity, the Ranger legged toward the ridge that overshadowed the holding to the south. He reached its flank and began slowly working up the rock-etched incline. Sweating, slipping on loose shale, he continued persistently upward, using his hands now to grab the stunted brush that scabbed the slope for support as the grade became steeper.

When finally he approached the crest, he bellied down, worming between outcroppings of rock. Breathing hard, he turned his head and looked back into the gulch—a chasm of darkness in which a small square gleamed faintly, a covered side window of the cabin. Around him, vague in the uncertain light, fragments of rock and patches of scrubby brush splotched the hogback. If the sharp-shooting jasper paid a return visit, he reflected with satisfaction, he'd be there to give him more than he bargained for.

He settled himself to wait, stretched out and relaxed, staring up at the silent legions of stars blinking overhead, through which, like a fiery spark, an occasional tiny meteorite flashed and died. Unbroken by quiet lay on the solitudes, broken abruptly by the flat unmistakable sprang of a Winchester further down ridge. He jerked to a sitting position, staring through the night. A segment of moon floated serenely above the ridges, its wan light laying a tracery shadow over the brush, and loose rock botched around. But he could detect no sign of movement.

Again, the whiplike crack of a rifleshot punched into his ears. Slowly, he began crawling in the direction of the sound, easing around misshapen fragments of rock, and skirting thorny mesquite. Once he pulled back hastily at the sound of a disturbed diamondback's warning rattle.

A third gunshot shattered the silence, very close now. He froze, then flattened out and slithered ahead. Not more than a few paces distant he glimpsed the form of a man— vague in the night—stretched out, Winchester cuddled to shoulder.

The rifle belched fire. By the powder flash he saw that the marksman was compactly built, broad-shouldered, and clad in rider's garb. Metal tinkled as the stranger ejected the empty shell and it dropped upon rock.

Nerves tight, Duane wormed closer. The rifle stabbed

fire again. The sound of movement muffled by the report, the Ranger jerked to his feet, took one long step and flung himself upon the outstretched form. He groped for the other's throat and—found he had a tiger by the tail. The chunky marksman was as hard-muscled and quick-moving as a mustang. He gasped at the impact of Duane's rangy form, then hunched his back.

Duane clung like a cougar, fingers digging into the muscular neck. With ease, it seemed, the other rolled, throwing him off balance. A knee pistoned into Duane's groin like a hard-driven wagon pole, and the other wrenched free as Duane grunted with agony, and slackened his grip.

The two men grappled, threshing over the ground, their legs flailing. Hooked fingers groped for Duane's eyes. He latched onto the fingers, levered them backward, and pressed his face against the stocky rider's shirted chest. His free fist bunched and smashed at his opponent's features, no more than a blur in the night.

Gulping air in sobbing gasps, the stranger latched onto the Ranger's hair, wrenching his head back, fighting desperately to break free. Still struggling with silent ferocity, they rolled downward over the rough ground interlocked, their writhing bodies cannoning into a boulder. Grunting and gasping, the frantic rider found Duane's windpipe, and his hard fingers compressed like the steel jaws of a trap.

Half-throttled now, blood salty on his lips, the Ranger fought to break the hold, conscious of a roaring in his ears, a red curtain clouding his eyes. Choking, he smashed at his assailant's features with savage short-arm jabs, experiencing a sudden, bitter exhilaration as the grip on his throat loosened and he felt the other's muscles relax.

Sucking air into his straining lungs, he continued blindly pounding with bloodied fists until, like a thunderclap, a crushing blow descended upon the back of his head. Consciousness left him in a blinding flash of light. He sprawled senselss over the slack form beneath him.

Long ages later, Duane groaned and stirred. His eyes

blinked open and he stared, uncomprehending, at a spread of stars. His brain fogged, he struggled to a sitting position, groaned again and clapped both hands to the back of his head as waves of pain surged over him. For a while he sat unmoving, nursing his bruised skull, striving to think coherently. Gradually, remembrance seeped back —the gunshots, the fight, the blow.

As the waves of pain subsided, his fingers, gingerly exploring, touched a swelling through his hair that seemed as big as a watermelon. There must have been a second man on the ridge he reflected—a man who'd ducked into the picture just as he'd mastered the chunky marksman, and clouted him with a gun butt.

He had just started to struggle to his feet when the glint of moonlight on metal caught his eye. Duane reached out and picked up the brass shell of an expended cartridge. A second and a third lay close to where they had been ejected from a Winchester. He gathered them up, stuffed them into a pants pocket. A moment later he was crossing the uneven terrain, swaying unsteadily. When at last he stumbled into the cabin he flopped gratefully onto the bed, and lay exhausted. Finally he sank into an uneasy sleep that was half stupor.

The sun was high and magpies clattered cheerfully around the eaves when the Ranger awoke the next morning. His throat felt as though he had been swallowing ashes, his head throbbed persistently and it seemed every muscle in his bruised body made aching complaint. Half-dazed, he blundered into the kitchen, stripped off his shirt and sloshed cold water over his head and torso.

Two steaming mugs of black coffee helped to clarify his thoughts. Duane remembered the empties he had picked up on the ridge. Fishing them out, he examined the bases. On each, the firing pin had struck practically on center. The two empties he had picked up at the scene of Murdoch's killing carried the indents off-center, which indicated the man he had battled the previous night wasn't Murdoch's bushwhacker. At least, he considered, that disposed of Welch's theory—there was more than one half-crazed prospector interested in the quarter-section.

XIII

There was no shooting that night or the next, and Buck Duane began to feel that his unknown assailants had decided he wouldn't scare. It was plain that they had really wanted to do no more than scare him. The hombre who had laid what was in all likelihood a steel barrel across his skull could have finished him right then and there, which strongly suggested they had no desire for the Murdoch place to become the focus of attention again because of another killing.

They had apparently just wanted him out of the way and a chance to continue digging. He would have gotten busy with a shovel himself. But he was restrained by the thought that Murdoch was too slick to move the ingots to a spot where they could be turned up by random digging.

There were a hundred spots in the rugged terrain within a mile of the cabin where buried gold would elude discovery until Doomsday. It was curious the ex-mine superintendent hadn't given his niece a clue to their location, knowing his associates were the type who would kill without a glimmer of a scruple. Murdoch had probably figured they'd never rub him out and forfeit a chance of locating the loot as long as he alone knew where it was hidden. And that, of course, had been a tragic miscalculation.

The soreness from the Ranger's own rough-and-tumble with the rider on the ridge had worn off, and the only reminder of the fracas was a slowly shrinking lump on the back of his head. It was still painful and he was in no amiable frame of mind when three riders jogged in—the town marshal, the granite-faced Carson and a tall rider with lean, leathery features and pale eyes bleak as lava knobs.

What now, wondered Duane, remembering the cowman's last visit. He sauntered forward to meet them as they peeled out of leather by the corral.

"Guess you're acquainted with these gents," said Welch. "Jim Carson rods the CCC, Lanky Larn'er his foreman."

Duane nodded at the two, who stood eying him impassively. "Well," he inquired, "what brought you up here?"

Welch looked uncomfortable. "Carson's having trouble with rustlers and—" he paused to clear his throat.

"Don't beat around the bush, Frosty," put in the cowman, with harsh impatience. "Tell this maverick I got a notion he's packing a sticky rope."

"Just hearing you say it is enough," Duane said, his anger rising. "It's a damned lie."

"Hold on now," exclaimed Welch quickly. "We can settle this peacefully. Carson filed a complaint and it's my duty to follow through. I've got no choice he claims his boys found sign of rustled stock, right in this gulch."

"Maybe he never heard of strays."

"I figured strays, but Carson's dead set on bracing you." Welch eyed the cowman. "All right, it's your move. Lay proof on the line, or withdraw your complaint."

"I'm sure we'll find proof," growled the rancher. He nodded to his foreman. "Poke around, Lanky. Maybe you'll turn up something."

Fuming, Duane watched the tall foreman stroll around the barn, eyes searching, kicking aside moldering pieces of equipment junked through the years. What was he expecting to find, wondered the Ranger—a freshskinned hide or a sacked side of beef? Carson was on unsure ground—and knew it. Just what did the tough old moseyhorn have in mind, filing a loco charge and dragging the marshal up into the hills?

Welch made a cigarette, his glance following the foreman. The rancher just stood unmoving, as though carved from rock.

The foreman finished his leisurely inspection and

ducked into the barn. The heads of the three men waiting outside swiveled when he backed out dragging two hides, so fresh that they hadn't began to stiffen. Duane glanced at Welch and saw that there was a look of dawning amazement in his eyes. Carson chuckled.

Without speaking, the tall foreman spread the hides, hair side up, then turned to his boss. "Rolled up," he said, "and stuck behind a bale of hay. The saddlebum is as guilty as hell."

With tight anger, Duane stared at the hides, each with the neat "CCC" brand burned through the hair. It was plain enough now. Carson had known all along the hides were there. He'd either had them planted or had been told they were hidden in the barn. On his previous visit, he'd warned that he always got what he wanted. Carson wanted him—Duane—off the Murdoch place and he was the type to whom the end always justified the means.

The Ranger had difficulty in restraining himself from rabbing Carson by the shoulders, forcing him to his knees, and beating the truth out of him.

"Those hides were planted!" he said quietly.

"I expected you to say that," retorted Carson, the ghost of a grin flitting around his tight lips. "Well, I guess that clears everything up, Frosty."

The marshal nodded grimly. Yanking a pair of handcuffs from a back pocket, he clamped them on Duane's wrists.

Lanky Larner rolled up the hides. "You'll need these for evidence," he drawled, and secured the cumbersome bundle behind the cantle of Welch's saddlehorse.

Carson walked up to the prisoner. "Maybe I should have brought a bunch of the boys and strung you up," he rasped.

"All right," Welch said. "That's enough. Taking him back to town is my job." He waited with his hands planted on his hips until Carson and his men mounted and rode off. Then when the sound of their horses' hoof-beats died, Welch fished out a key, unlocked the cuffs and dropped them into his pocket.

"Aren't you taking chances with a dangerous rustler?" said Duane, with dreary humor.

"Not when I got your gun," returned the lawman. "Let's chew this over."

They both hunkered against the barn.

"I hope you realize it was a frameup!" declared the Ranger. "Two steers! Could I eat the meat? If not, where would I peddle it?"

"Carson rods the biggest spread in the valley," said Welch. "Why would he frame you?"

"To get me off this place," Duane said. He related the story of Carson's former visit, the cowmen's offer of a handsome bonus if Miss Stokes could be persuaded to sell, and his rage at being turned down.

Then the Ranger told Welch about the shooting from the ridge and the midnight fracas. "I've got a bump as big as a camel's hump on the back of my head to prove it," he concluded. "Apparently there's two outfits hellbent to run me off—Carson's CCC and the bunch who beefed Murdoch."

"Talk of buried gold is percolating all over now," Welch said, his voice tinged with resentment. "Mrs. Purdy claims Siegler's dickering with the schoolma'am." He snorted. "All acting as crazy as popcorn on a hot stove."

"Why the shooting?" said Duane.

"Carson's punchers roostering you. That old moseyhorn's sure on the prod." He came back to his feet. "I guess we'd better start back."

"Do you intend to jug me!" Duane was unable to keep anger out of his voice.

"What choice have I got?" said Welch. "Carson's filed a complaint and dug up evidence." He nodded at the bulky bundle roped behind his cantle and wrinkled his nose. "Mighty odorous evidence, too. Failing bail, the sheriff holds you for the circuit judge. But the odds are you'll never face trial. Carson saw me clamp handcuffs on you and I'm pretty sure the old wart hog's satisfied. He doesn't think you'll come back here. When the case comes up I'll stake my saddle he won't prosecute."

Sheriff Harrigan was proud of his jail, mainly because it provided concrete evidence of the voters' wisdom in electing him to office—and presented a solid argument for reelection. A long, low adobe, it sat behind the courthouse in Cochrane. Its walls were four feet thick and its steel-barred cells escape-proof, and it hadn't cost the taxpayers one red cent, beyond materials, due to the sheriff's happy inspiration to use prison labor in its construction.

Before the week was out, Buck Duane had an unexpected visitor—the unctuous, bland-featured Julius Siegler. The gaunt-looking storekeeper was garbed in the rusty frock coat, dark pants and plug hat he usually reserved for such ceremonial occasions as funerals.

When he padded unobtrusively down the jail corridor, darting apprehensive glances into the cells, he reminded the prisoner of nothing so much as an itinerant preacher slipping into a house of ill-fame. Reaching Duane's cell, he paused, peering between the bars.

"So you've fallen on evil days, young man," he observed.

"I would be the last to deny that," Duane said, regarding the storekeeper curiously. "But I hope you didn't come here just to remind me of it. I'm not ready to be planted."

Siegler's smooth features contorted into a melancholy smile. "When that time arrives," he said, "may I suggest that nowhere would the ceremonies be handled more efficiently than at Hertzburg."

"That's a pleasant thought," rejoined the Ranger, his puzzlement increasing. "But don't tell me you dropped in to drum up business."

"No." Siegler's countenance twisted into a wintry smile. "I came to arrange for your release—on bail."

Duane stared at him incredulously. What possible reason could the old carrion crow have for helping him out of jail? "You'll go bail—for me?"

"Under certain conditions," Siegler said.

"What conditions?" Duane asked suspiciously. It was difficult to imagine Julius Siegler doing a stranger—or anyone, for that matter—a favor without prospect of personal profit.

"Perfectly reasonable conditions." The storekeeper laced long fingers across his middle and his guileless eyes dwelt mediatively upon the man behind the bars. "I am dickering with Miss Stokes for purchase of the Murdoch place. It has come to my knowledge that several men— quite illegally—are digging on the property. It is essential that they be closely watched."

Duane thought fast. It was plain that the old moneybags had somehow obtained knowledge of the hidden gold and was scared that it might be removed before he obtained possession of the quarter-section. "You know why they're digging?" he said.

"I have a notion," admitted the storekeeper cautiously.

"I see. Have you any objections to spelling it out for me?"

"I've reason to believe there's something valuable buried there," returned the other quickly. "I wish to explore the possibility."

"Why brace me?"

"You are the only person who is well acquainted with the property. Furthermore, it is necessary to cross the CCC range to reach it. Carson, who owns the ranch is a belligerent type. He persists in regarding all interlopers as rustlers. Various persons I have hired have been fired upon in the past and run off."

"So you ran out of volunteers and got the notion that if you bailed me out I might be willing to risk getting riddled with lead. Is that it?"

Siegler frowned, ignoring the question. "I need a trustworthy man," he went on, "who will advise me immediately if anything unusual transpires."

"It's a deal!" said Duane promptly. Anything, he thought, to get out of this hole.

"Excellent!" Relief showed plain in the storekeeper's

tone. He was clearly tortured by the thought that someone would get to that gold first and ace him out of a $150,000 bounty, reflected Duane, as his gaze followed Siegler's decorous exit. Now he was due to sweat awhile himself, waiting to see if the storekeeper went through with the deal.

Hours passed, and it was early afternoon before the jailer reappeared, a ring of keys jingling on his belt. In no haste, he fitted one to the cell gate, swung it open. "Rattle your hocks," he growled. "Sheriff craves a word with you."

He steered his prisoner out of the jail, along a covered dog-trot, and through a rear door of the courthouse. Their footsteps echoed down a wide corridor, along which closed doors were spaced, each neatly lettered with the name of a county official. The last, near the glass-panelled front doors, carried the words, WALTER HARRIGAN, *County Sheriff.*

The beefy jailer turned the handle and nudged his prisoner inside. Buck found himself in a high-ceilinged room. Four straightback chairs were line up against the far wall. A rack, beyond them, held a row of lethal-looking shot guns. The opposite wall was plastered with "Wanted" notices. At the end of the room, by two narrow front windows, a bull of a man sat hunched at a rolltop desk, a stogie stuck between his lips. At the prisoner's entrance he swung around.

Sheriff Harrigan was graying and going to fat. His florid features reflected the meaningless affability of the elected official and his belly lapped over his belt. But a strong sweet of jaw was plain beneath the flesh jowls.

"Well, Duane," he drawled, reaching for a sheet lying on the desk, "you're in luck." He eyed the sheet, intoned, "Order for the release of Buck Duane, signed by Judge Nabors. Bail set at two hundred fifty dollars, furnished by Julius Siegler, Hertzburg." Benevolently, he added, "Now keep out of trouble!"

"I never was in trouble," retorted the prisoner. "I was framed."

The sheriff smiled resignedly. "Sure," he said. "All you got to do is convince a jury."

XV

A quick trip to the old Murdoch place showed Duane that several men—he guessed at least three—had been digging extensively on the property.

Since Siegler had eased him out of jail for the express purpose of keeping cases on the Murdoch place, Buck Duane felt the storekeeper was at least entitled to some kind of an immediate report, even if Siegler would not like the news. He decided to head right back to The Emporium.

The Siegler he found enthroned in his office, amid accounts, catalogs and cash books, was very different from the self-affacing, benevolent funeral director. There was little guilelessness in Siegler's sharp eyes and an edge to his greeting.

Duane swept some price lists off a chair by the desk, dropped onto it and told him of the digging.

Pulling abstractedly at his long nose, Siegler listened to the story with frowning attention. He appeared pleased, rather than annoyed, by news of the continued digging. "That certainly confirms Silas Leeson's claim," he murmured.

"Leeson's claim?" questioned Duane.

"Silas suspected there might be something of worth buried on the quarter-section," he explained hastily. "I meant to tell you that when we had our talk."

Just how much did the storekeeper really know, wondered Duane. Aloud, he asked, "Is it your idea I should get back out there?"

Worrying the end of a pencil with sharp teeth, Siegler thought it over. "Perhaps you had better remain in town," he finally decided. "The interlopers—have apparently taken flight and I expect to learn, any day, that Miss

Stokes has accepted the very generous officer I made for the property. Immediately I assume possession, I intend to hire as many men as I can round up—to dig. You will supervise their efforts."

Playing up to his role of saddlebum, Duane reminded his new "boss," "I've got to eat—and sleep. You forgot the county stopped supplying me with board and lodging?"

"I'll instruct the hotel clerk to allot a room and Ah Wang at the restaurant to provide meals." The storekeeper's tone held obvious reluctance.

The old tightwad certainly hated to pay out, thought Duane and, from sheer perversity, decided to prod further, "A man gets thirsty," he observed pointedly.

"A wise man drinks water—Nature's nectar," said Siegler, with a wintry smile. "In Hertzburg there is no lack of water. If you are dissatisfied, young man, I can always revoke the bail bond."

The old fellow didn't have him over the barrel exactly. But going back to jail would not have helped him. He smiled tightly and rose. "Well—it's all right with me if you want me to drink your health in water," he observed, and headed for the street.

Three days passed and no further word came from the storekeeper. Duane was sitting in a relaxed position in one of the shabby rockers that decorated the hotel lobby, killing time, when he heard the distant shriek of an engine whistle. Hat tilted over his eyes, he continued to half-doze, aware that the deep tolling of an engine bell from the direction of the railway depot meant that the mixed passenger-freight had arrived.

From beneath the hatbrim, he glimpsed not long afterwards the flirt of skirts. Duane straightened in his seat and blinked with surprise. Mildred Stokes, composed and correct as always, was crossing the lobby with a brisk, decisive stride. At her heels tagged a plump Mexican girl in red skirt and white camiso, a filmy rebozo swathed around head and shoulders. Both girls packed traveling bags.

Duane rose quickly, stepped forward and intercepted the school ma'am. "Welcome back, Miss Stokes," he said. "If I had known—"

She stopped and stared at him in surprise. "I thought you were watching my property," she said, her voice accusing.

"There's been trouble out there."

"But you gave me to understand you wouldn't leave the place unguarded—no matter how much trouble you had to contend with."

It was plain, Duane reflected, that she knew nothing of what had transpired on the lonely quarter-section.

"There's a great deal that needs to be explained," he said. "There are times when a man has no choice."

"There's no need for explanations," she assured him sharply. She tried to push past him, but he blocked her path.

"You sold—to Siegler?"

"No!" she snapped. "Not that he hasn't been pestering me to sell. Pinkerton's, the detective agency, have also been plaguing me—for permission to dig on the property." Her prim lips tightened. "You told me yourself that—well, that you were almost sure my uncle, had hidden gold there. The newspaper you showed me—"

"I'm more sure than ever now. If you'll just listen—"

"I intend to investigate personally, and I need no assistance," she told him stiffly. "Come, Juana!"

"You're not going into the hills alone," said the Ranger.

"I have a companion!"

"You'll both be heading straight into trouble—big trouble."

"Poppycock!" she cried. "I am quite capable of taking care of myself. Now perhaps you will excuse me."

Baffled, Buck Duane returned to his chair and sat watching the schoolma'am and her Mexican friend—or servant, he couldn't guess which—book a room and head for the stairway.

He could not be sure, of course. But the possibility could

not be ruled out that gold fever had infected Murdoch's niece. Siegler's efforts to buy the quarter-section and Pinkerton's eagerness to dig had perhaps convinced her that wealth awaited the first person to get busy with a shovel. What seemed just as likely, however, was the simple fact that there were women who could go into a sudden rage when they had the mistaken idea that a man should never disappoint them, even when he had no choice. His cogitations were interrupted by the reappearance of Mildred Stokes on the stairs. She hurried down and moved purposefully toward him.

"We need a guide to the property," she said, her voice still a trifle brusque, but no longer angrily accusing. "Are you available?"

"Yes—but only because I couldn't go on respecting myself if I let *any* two women go out there alone."

"Then please rent two saddlehorses and a pack animal, to carry supplies. Then meet us at the store."

Within the hour, they pulled out—Duane ahead, leading a well-laden pack mule; Mildred Stokes, enveloped in overalls, tailing him and Juana in the rear, her bare legs dangling on each side of her mount. They'd scarcely hit the river trail when dust smoked ahead and a buckboard came into view, bumping and bouncing behind a team stretched out at full gallop. Duane didn't have to guess who held the lines.

Rosita Carson hauled the sweatplastered broncs to a halt when the vehicle drew close. Her red lips curved with amusement as she sat quietly watching the riders file past.

"So now you have a harem!" she taunted Duane, ignoring Miss Stokes' first startled, then enraged look. Concealing his irritation, the Ranger stared straight ahead.

Dead and deserted, Murdoch's place lay sweltering in the sun when they rode in. Trail-stained and saddlesore, the girls wearily dragged into the cabin and close the door behind them. Duane busied himself unloading the pack mule, stacking supplies on the porch. Among the schoolma'am's purchases was a double-barrelled shotgun.

159

He chuckled, thinking she was the type who would use it. When he was through, he knuckled the door. Mildred Stokes, now spruce in white blouse and dark skirt, opened it.

"Would you like me to pack in water and wood?" he inquired.

"No," she informed him crisply. "But I suggest you loose the pack in the corral." She opened the handbag dangling from a wrist, extracted a leather purse and carefully counted out five silver dollars. "That, I believe, is the agreed amount for your services. That should take care of it."

Duane stood very still, eying the lengthening shadows and wondering how many pairs of eyes were casing them through the gathering gloom. "Won't cost you a dollar, ma'am," he said, with mock humility in his voice.

Then, one by one, he spun the coins in the sagebrush a few feet from where they were standing. He had a sudden impulse to take her firmly by the shoulders and shake her, then bring his lips down hard on hers. But he restrained himself.

Sudden anger flamed in Mildred Stokes' eyes. "I insist that you leave at once. Juana and I are quite capable of looking after ourselves. And, remember, we have a shotgun."

So did Murdoch,, thought the Ranger, but it didn't help any. Mildred raised the gun and trained it on him. "I'm very serious about what I just said. I want you to go, at once."

Jogging through the thickening darkness back to town, Duane couldn't keep his thoughts off the irrationally impulsive green-eyed girl he'd left back in the hills with her plump Mexican companion. Common sense told him there was less chance of chasing the desperados who had held up the gold shipment away from Murdoch's place than scaring bees away from honey.

They'd killed at least five men to get that gold and it was a sure thing they wouldn't quit as long as a chance of retrieving it remained. Mildred Stokes was sitting on a

160

powder keg. But Duane realized she had no intention of returning to town where he might shake some sense into her.

He returned the rented saddlehorses, ate in The Ritz—at Siegler's expense—and decided to let one night go by, feeling convinced Mildred was in considerably less danger than a man would have been. The gold-seekers would see in her no real obstacle to their plans, and would not try to scare her off immediately. And they'd know that if they harmed her the whole town would be in an uproar and a dozen posses would be after them with as many nooses.

When he awoke the next morning, the sun already rimmed the eastern horizon. He'd omitted to pull down the window shade and a broad white shaft spanned the hotel room, patching the far wall.

Sluiced off and shaved, Buck Duane dropped down the creaky treads of the stairway and headed for the hash-house. Little activity showed on Main Street, beyond a store clerk or two sweeping off fronts and washing windows, and the wrinkled Mexican, the zanzero, refilling water barrels set along the plankwalk. He saw Welch, always an early riser, step out of the eating house, building a smoke.

The frenzied beat of hooves on the plank bridge that spanned the creek reached his ears, like the tattoo on a distant drum. Someone in an all-fired hurry, he thought, then tensed with surprise at sight of the pack mule he had left with the girls. Stretched out at full gallop, it came down the wide, sandy street, neck outstretched, tail streaming.

Riding bareback was the Mexican girl, clutching its flying mane with one hand, belaboring it with a switch with the other. Her long hair in disorder, her rumpled red skirt displaying bare brown legs, she frantically lashed the mule, her features contorted with terror.

Welch ran out into the street as she allowed the mule to halt. It stood gaunted and trembling, blowing hard with lowered head. Duane, dashing up behind the marshal, saw that the girl's bare legs were scratched and scoured by brush.

"They shoot! They keel!" gasped the girl. Then she fainted, dropping slack across the mule's withers.

XVI

Between them, the town marshal and Buck Duane eased the slumped Mexican girl off the jaded mule, and carried her into the lobby of the hotel.

"We'll need a doctor," Duane said, when they lowered her into a rocker, and she fell back limply on the shabby cushions.

"There's no doctor closer than Cochrane," Welch said, his face set in tight lines. The girl's eyes were closed and her dark hair straggled in disorder over her swarthy face.

"I'd better get Ma Purday," Welch decided. "She'll know what to do."

He was gone barely five minutes when the widow hustled in with a rustle of skirts. Ma Purdy's quick glance strayed over Juana's grumpled garb, and the lacerations on her brown legs. She pickedup a limp wrist and checked the girl's pulse. Then her beady eyes fixed on Duane. "You took her out to Murdoch's, with Miss Stokes?" It was more accusation than question.

Duane nodded.

"If there's anything to the talk that's floating around, that's no place for a woman."

"Miss Stokes was determined to take over the cabin," Duane said. "She forced me to leave at the point of a gun. I wouldn't be telling you this if I wasn't twenty times as concerned as you are."

Ma Purdy spoke to the clerk, who had left the desk and was standing at Welch's side. "We need a room, George, and a crock of hot water. Now you," she turned to Duane, "pack her upstairs."

The Ranger gathered up the unconscious girl in his arms and followed Ma's stringy form up the stairway. She consulted a key tab and threw open the door of a room on the second floor. Duane deposited Juana on the bed, and remained for a moment staring down at her, hoping she would open her eyes and begin to talk. But when that seemed unlikely he strode out of the room.

In the lobby he rejoined Marshal Welch. "She may not be able to speak for an hour or more. We've got to get to the cabin fast."

"I know. I'll swear in a posse, and—"

"That'll take time."

"A half hour I'm afraid."

"And Miss Stokes may not even be alive. Hell, I'm riding, right now."

"Makes sense," said Welch. "Let's get started."

Nothing seemed amiss when they jogged into the holding. Magpies still chattered among the weeds sprouting from the cabin roof, and humming birds darted the dapple sunlight for flashing jewels. They peeled out of leather in front of the cabin and Duane saw that the door was closed. Fearful of what lay behind it, he hurried inside. Everything appeared to be in order—the Rochester lamp stood exactly in the center of the table, the two chairs with laced rawhide seats were drawn up precisely on either side, and the bookcase was no longer grayed by a thick layer of dust.

He stepped quickly into the bedroom. The bed was neatly made. A flannel nightgown lay carefully folded on a chair beside it and a pair of furry slippers was set underneath.

There appeared to be nothing amiss in the kitchen, either. Perplexed, he moved outside. Welch, hunkered against an upright of the porch, was drawing on a cigarette.

"I can't understand it!" Duane exclaimed. "You'd think she had just stepped out for a moment."

The marshal said nothing, just pointed. Following the direction of his finger, Duane glimpsed an overalled form busily digging beyond a clumb of mesquite, two hundred

163

paces or more beyond the well. "I'll be damned!" he muttered.

At their approach, Mildred Stokes straightened, brushing back wisps of auburn hair from her damp forehead. "Well?" she challenged.

"We thought we might find you lying here dead," said Duane.

"Dead!" the schoolma'am seemed amused. "That fool Juana, I suppose. There was firing during the night and some bullets hit the cabin. She became hysterical and rode off. I shouted after her, begging her to be sensible, but she paid no attention."

"Weren't you frightened, too, ma'am?" inquired Welch.

"I'm certainly not going to be driven off my property by a few random shots," she replied.

"Not when you're searching for buried treasure," put in Duane deadpan.

"Is that a crime?" Miss Stokes bristled. "This is my property and I have every right to dig wherever and whenever I please."

"Ma'am," put in the marshal bleakly, "maybe you should think twice about that. The shots could have been intended as a warning. Next time this night-shooting hombre may feel the same way about you as he did about your uncle. He may shoot to kill. This is no place for a woman—alone."

"That's for me to decide," she cried. "Right now, you're trespassing. I'll thank you to leave." The two men exchanged glances. Welch raised his shoulders in a fatalistic gesture. The stubborn Mildred Stokes strode away, stopped at a sandy spot and began turning the earth over again.

"I never saw a stubborner woman!" breathed Welch, with soft vehemence.

"What do you think should be done about it?" said Duane, watching the girl as she awkwardly wielded the heavy shovel.

"Nothing!" barked the marshal.

"We can't just leave her here now. You know that as well as I do."

"We sure can't run her off," Welch said. "This is her property."

Disgust written plain on his face, he began trudging back to the cabin. Duane followed him.

When they reached their horses, the marshal stepped into leather. Duane made no effort to mount.

"Who's stepping on your shirttail?" inquired Welch irately.

"I'm sticking around."

"For what?"

"Maybe I can make her change her mind."

"You sure got my good wishes," growled the lawman, and raised his reins.

Buck Duane stood watching Welch pull away. The marshal, he considered, was certainly very angry. But perhaps he couldn't be blamed for feeling the way he did. They'd pushed their ponies hard, through a long, tiring ride, not knowing what they would find at its end, and the only thanks they'd received for their efforts had been a slap in the face.

The school ma'am had a mind of her own, all right. But the Ranger had to admit she was spunky, too. Few women—or men for that matter—would stick it out, alone, in an isolated cabin, menaced by unseen enemies throwing lead in the night.

The Ranger stripped the gear off his mount, watered Bullet and loosed him in the corral. Later he hunkered in the shade of the porch, smoking and eying the quite mad girl as she toiled out in the sunglare.

Near noon, she walked back to the cabin. She looked hot, tired and annoyed. It was not until she'd disgustedly thrown the shovel aside that she became aware of Duane's presence.

"What are you doing here?" Mildred Stokes demanded.

"I just thought I'd stick around."

"I don't need you—or any man—around."

"I'm afraid you've got no choice," he said.

With an exasperated glance, she brushed past him and entered the cabin, firmly closing the door. He heard the bar drop into place.

After awhile, Duane came to his feet, drifted around to the barn, found a patch of shade and stretched out in siesta.

When he awoke, the sun was beginning to arc toward the west. He saw a moving form, out amid the waste of scrub and rock. Mildred Stokes, he reflected, was certainly dead-set on locating the buried ingots.

When she dragged in toward sundown he had the coffee pot bubbling on the stove and chuck sizzling in a frying pan. Beyond an angrily contemptuous glance, the girl ignored him. Plainly sore-muscled from digging, she sank into a chair and accepted in frigid silence the plate of bacon and beans he placed before her. Setting the steaming coffee pot on the table, he pulled up a chair and began eating his own supper.

Her plate emptied, Mildred Stokes sipped her coffee, looking at the Ranger with angry green eyes. "Mr. Duane," she said forcefully. "You must realize that you can't stay—overnight."

"Why not?" he inquired, between mouthfuls.

"It certainly wouldn't be proper."

"I took a couple of blankets out into the barn."

"Don't you realize," she flung back at him, "that I prefer to be *alone*—that is, if you don't mind?"

"And don't you realize," he mimicked tolerantly, "that the hombres who stole those ingots are still ghosting around. As Welch said, if they can't scare you off, they may decide to shoot you."

"Nonsense!" she snapped.

Duane shrugged. It was plain that the girl was obsessed by a golden vision. She could think of nothing but buried ingots—and the fortune that awaited her if she could uncover them.

Throughout the evening she endured his presence with chilled indifference. With darkness, he wandered out to the barn and squatted against its clapboards, smoking.

Gradually the gloom thickened, and a chill breeze soughed across the ridges and rustled dead brush, and a night bird circled with harsh chittering.

Duane came erect, fingered his way inside the darkened barn and found his blankets. At a thought, he moved outside again and slid his Winchester out of the boot. Trouble was brewing, he could feel it in his bones. The distant spang of a rifle shot stirred him into wakefulness. He sat up, fumbling for his boots. From somewhere out in the night, another, and another gunshot spluttered like firecrackers. Grabbing the Winchester, Duane slid outside.

From the ridge to the south, a lance of flame licked through the darkness. He heard the drone of a slug that plonked into the timbers of the cabin. A second gun opened up, from the west. Crouching, he ran around to the front of the cabin. The door was firmly secured. He hammered it frantically with a fist. It opened hesitantly. Dim in the starlight, he saw Mildred Stokes, a robe wrapt around her. The remaining window shattered, the bullet buzzing across the room like an angry hornet.

"We've got trouble," he called out, and stepped inside. Slamming the door, he dropped the bar into place.

"They're only trying to scare us," insisted the girl, now invisible in the darkened cabin. But he detected a quaver in her tone.

"They might just prefer to kill us," he snapped, and ducked instinctively as another slug whined through the broken window. "Get down!"

A chair clattered as he stumbled over it, moving to a spot from which he could watch both windows. Beyond the bedroom window, a flicker of red caught his eye. He sniffed. There was the scent of burning on the air. He ran into the bedroom and glanced out through the window frame, still edged with ragged fragments of gypsum.

"Good Lord!" he exclaimed. "The barn's afire."

XVII

Quickly, Buck Duane smashed splinters of gypsum projecting from the frame flat with the barrel of his Winchester, and squeezed through. When he hurried around the angle of the cabin, the barn came into full view. Burning wood crackled and yellow-red tongues of flame licked up the heat-shrunk clapboards. Snorting in terror, Bullet raced around the corral. Dim in the shadows beyond, Duane glimpsed the form of a moving man. Without pausing, he levered a shell into the breech and swung the Winchester to his shoulder. He squeezed the trigger, ejected the empty shell, fired again.

The barn was doomed. One glance made that plain. Already, the fire had taken hold with a deep-throated, menacing roar. Waves of heat beat at him as flames began to curl high above the roof. The Ranger quashed an impulse to run for water, knowing that the few buckets he could have packed from the well would be useless.

First he had to get Bullet out of danger. He ran for the corral. By the pole gate, the horse's rig lay on the ground. He snatched up the bridle, ducked inside, slipped it over the terrified animal's ears, secured the throat latch, and let it out.

The horse out of harm's way, Duane stood watching the conflagration, frustrated at his own impotence. Sparks showered as the roof crashed, dragging the blazing walls down with it. A column of fire now shot skyward, smoke ballooning above it like a vast mushroom, obscuring the stars. Suddenly, he became aware that Mildred Stokes was standing beside him, still wrapped in her robe, the shotgun grasped in both hands. The garish light of the fire reflected in her green eyes as she stared absorbed at the blazing barn.

"Was it deliberately set?" There was no tremor in her clear voice.

"I'm sure it was," he replied. "I threw a couple of shots at the jasper who put a torch to it."

As sparks showered high, she threw an apprehensive glance at the cabin behind them. "Is it going to spread?"

"I don't think so!" he assured her. "There's not much to burn, outside the cabin, and that's roofed with six inches of soddy."

They stood in silence, watching the flames gradually die down. The old shanty barn had been nothing more than a shell, considered Duane—just walls and roof. Soon it was reduced to a square of glowing debris, amidst which smoldering timbers still crackled. The air was thick with floating ash and rank with the acrid stench of burning. Then Duane noticed that the desultory firing from the night had died away, too.

"Guess we better get back inside," he said. "Well, they made it plain."

"That they want me out," returned Mildred bleakly. "Well, they won't get rid of me so easily."

"Talking that way makes no sense at all," the Ranger said with tight exasperation. He took her arm and began steering her back to the cabin.

Inside, he routed out an old slicker, tore it in half and covered the two smashed windows. This done, he lit the Rochester lamp. "You can go back to bed," he told her. "They'll probably leave us in peace—until tomorrow night."

"And you?" She eyed him uncertainly.

"I'm staying—right here!"

She bit back a protest and stepped into the bedroom, still packing the shotgun. He chuckled silently when he heard the sound of a chair back being jammed beneath a door knob, and sank into the upholstered rocker. Yawning, he reached and turned out the lamp, dozed off—and awoke in darkness. Moving to the window, he yanked down the oilskin shading it. Outside, dawn showed wan and gray. Tenuous fingers of light wavered across the sky, erasing the stars.

His muscles stiff, Duane drifted into the kitchen, stuffed kindling into the stove and spilled water from a bucket into

169

the coffee pot. He was mixing flapjack batter and the coffee had begun to perk when Mildred Stokes walked in, a picture of spruceness, from the smoothly-coiled plaits of her auburn hair, through white blouse and dark skirt, down to button shoes. No one, he thought, would have guessed that she had spent half the night dodging lead.

She favored him with a cool nod and sat down in a chair by the window.

"Well," he asked, "did you have any second thoughts about sticking around?"

"Why should I?"

He shrugged. "You've forgotten the shooting, the burning barn? If you weren't so blind to all reason you'd pull out."

"And give those bandits a free hand? Never!"

"They'll be back!"

"And I'll be ready! Remember, I have a gun, too."

"I'm very much afraid," he told her soberly, "you'd never have a chance to use it."

Breakfast over, Buck Duane left the dishes for her to wash and wandered outside. He wanted to be alone, to figure out a course of action. It was plain that the obdurate Mildred Stokes could never be pried away from the Murdoch place as long as hope remained of recovering the looted ingots—and it was equally plain that their mysterious assailants would never stop for the same reason. And there were indications that the attackers were losing patience. At first they'd contented themselves with random shooting. Now they'd burned down the barn. Would the cabin be next?

Duane drifted around to where the barn had stood. Now all that remained was a sooted square, cumbered by a few half-consumed timbers, from which tiny tendrils of smoke still curled. He remembered the skulking form at which he had thrown lead, and probably missed! For no good reason, he wandered past the smoking debris, over ground cumbered with loose rock and stunted brush. Suddenly he jerked back on his heels at sight of a form in puncher garb, sprawled unmoving, face downward on the rugged ground.

The dead rider was tall and stringy. He was clad in gray shirt and corduroys, the bottoms thrust into spurred high boots. A broad gunbelt was buckled around his waist and a dented can lay by one limp hand. Easing closer, Duane saw that the shirt, between the dead man's shoulder blades, was stiff with dried blood, and a neat hole gaped where a bullet had punched through. So, by a streak of luck, he'd tagged the firebug. Bending, he picked up the can, sniffed. Coal oil. That banished all doubt. He rolled the body over, and almost gasped with surprise as he stared down at the slack features of Lanky Larner, the CCC foreman.

He had been wrong all the time, he mused. It was the CCC, not the looters, that was hellbent to clear all interlopers off the Murdoch place. Why? Could Carson, the cowman be on the track of the ingots, too? Following Murdoch's killing, and the discovery of Si Leeson's battered body in the alley beside the saloon, loose talk had been circulating all over town regarding buried treasure on the quarter-section. Likely, it had reached Carson's ears, and the rancher had decided to bull his way into the gold hunt.

It was more than puzzling, but one thing was sure—he had to get down to Hertzburg and inform the marshal. Welch would probably know how to handle it. He'd better leave the corpse where it was. There was no spare pony on which to bring it to town, and Mildred Stokes would just have to stomach a dead body lying around. He felt that she was tough enough to take it.

When Duane headed back to the cabin, she was just emerging, overall-clad.

"You're getting your wish," he told her. "There's something important I've got to see about in town. I'll be back before sundown."

"Don't hurry on my account," Mildred told him unconcernedly. She picked up the shovel.

Seated at his scarred desk, Town Marshal Welch listened impassively while Buck Duane told of the firing of the barn, the shooting in the night, and his discovery of the CCC foreman's body with the empty coal oil can.

When he was through, Welch grunted irritably, "That girl's sure stirring up a peck of trouble."

"She's simply standing up for her rights!" said Duane. "Carson's the troublemaker, I'd say. You should slap an arson charge on him."

"You figure I could make it stick?" The marshal's face was grim, but there was a trace of sardonic humor in his voice. "Cal's the biggest cowman in the valley. He heads the Cattlemen's Protective."

"That hardly gives him the right to fire a neighbor's barn?" Buck Duane pointed out. "Hell, you could make a try at it."

"I guess I'll have to. In view of what you've told me, I'm dutybound to brace the old buffalo," agreed the marshal, with scant enthusiasm.

When the buildings of the CCC came into view beneath the cottonwoods that flanked them like lofty sentinels the spread gave Duane the impression of being as big as Hertzburg. The ranchhouse, a long, rambling rock-and-adobe, was built around a central patio. Slit windows, barred with Spanish grillwork, and a low parapet that bordered the flat roof, gave the impression of a fort. Maybe a fort had been needed when Carson first drove a herd into the valley, thought Duane. Around the house lay a blotch of buildings —a long adobe bunkhouse, with lean-to cookshack, a big barn, a blacksmith shop, a stable and a wagon shed. A windmill clunked and whirled fitfully.

The big spread seemed empty when the two rode into the yard. A fat man, in singlet and greasy pants, emptied a bucket of water through the cookhouse door; a solitary puncher mucked out the stable. No one else appeared to be around, until Duane saw Carson's chunky form, slacked in an old rocker, set on the gallery that fronted the house. Nearby, his daughter, in crisp ginghams, occupied another rocker. She was busily knitting. The sight of the fiery Rosita engaged in such a humdrum household task caused the Ranger to smile to himself. So there was another, more domestic side, to her character.

They dismounted at the water trough, tied their mounts, with the spare pony Welch had brought alone to pack Lanky's body to town.

The weathered old rancher watched them poker-faced as they plowed through the dust of the yard.

"Howdy, Cal," greeted the marshal.

Carson nodded brusquely, then turned to Duane. "How is it you ain't in jail?" he asked.

"Out on bail," the Ranger grinned at him. "I never belonged there, as you well know."

Carson snorted. "I'll forget how I feel about it for a moment—or try to. Rest your legs anyway." He switched his attention to the lawman. "What brought you out here, Frosty?"

"A killing!" replied the marshal. "Lanky, your foreman, was beefed last night, firing the Murdoch barn."

Carson stared at him for a moment in stunned disbelief, too appalled by the new to say anything in reply.

"The law calls it arson," put in Duane. "There was shooting, too—at a girl."

Rosita recovered from the shock faster than her father.

"Not the green-eyed one, the schoolma'am?" she asked.

"Just what do you know about that burning, Cal?" asked Welch.

"Lanky knew I wanted that gulch cleared. Murdoch ran off tresspassers with a shotgun. Now he's buzzard bait, rustler scum skulk around there like coyotes around a carcase."

"So Lanky overplayed his hand?" .persisted the marshal.

"And you hope to pin it on me!" Carson shrugged.

"Go right ahead! A cowman has got a right to keep his range clean."

"Guess I'll chew it over with the sheriff," said Welch, and rose. Duane saw that he wasn't over-anxious to antagonize the rancher.

"When you see the sheriff, tell him to quash charges

against Duane." The heads of the three men swivelled at the sound of Rosita's voice.

"You plumb crazy, girl?" spluttered her father.

"Not too crazy to watch Lanky and Willis beef two prime steers and skin them out, down by the creek," she retorted. "Or to wonder why Willis packed the hides up to the hills."

"You been chewing loco weed," snorted Cal Carson.

"I can lead you to the carcasses, or what's left of them," the dark-haired girl said coolly to her perplexed father.

XVIII

It was near noon. A blazing sun flayed Wildcat Gulch and the surrounding hills simmered under its blasting rays, the ridges quivering through undulating heat waves. Frosty Welch had picked up the body of the CCC foreman and headed back to town.

Buck Duane squatted in the shade of the porch, watching Mildred Stokes moving about among clumped mesquite with her shovel. Queer what a fever for gold could do, he mused. Even a steer had sense enough to seek shelter from the sun at midday, but here was a girl, unused to hard labor, slaving like a convict on a rock pile, with blistered hands and aching bach. Chasing ghost gold.

One hundred and fourteen ingots, scaling twenty-seven pounds apiece, a ton and a half of metal. The renegades must have discovered that burying that much gold was quite a chore, even for four men. And it would have been a tougher chore for Murdoch, alone, to move the loot to another cache. He would have been compelled to handle the job under cover of darkness. Daylight would have revealed his trickery to his partners, probably keeping cases on him from the hills around. Dig another hole in the rocky ground, move almost a ton dead weight, bury it and cover it, all between dusk and dawn. An almost impossible chore for one man.

Possibly, reflected Duane, Murdoch hadn't reburied the ingots. Possibly he'd just moved them. But that didn't make sense either. They would have been discovered if they had been left above ground. The quarter-section now had been pretty well combed over—one hundred and fourteen gold bricks would stand out like a boil on a bald head. Murdoch had been shrewd—smart enough to outfox them all.

Mildred was moving in, and he could see by her dragging steps that she was tuckered out. She dropped the shovel by the porch, wearily mounted the wooden steps and dipped a drink from the ola. Then she sagged down against the front of the cabin. For the first time she looked at Duane with what seemed a bid for sympathy in her eyes.

"It's curious your uncle didn't give you *some* notion as to where you'd find the gold," the Ranger commented.

She raised her shoulders hopelessly. Her eyes held a new expression of warmth now. "He was always vague," she said. "He never went beyond hinting at great wealth, enough to keep me in luxury for the rest of my life. Actually, he wrote very seldom and I never met him in person. He wrote mostly about his ranch. Ranch!" She laughed with bitter scorn. "A waste of rocks and scrub!"

"Did he ever mention any special features of the ranch?" prompted Duane.

"No," she returned thoughtfully, "except perhaps the well. He seemed awfully proud of his well. He said he had the sweetest water in Camino County and that when I inherited the place I was to be sure and clean it out regularly—as though I would know how!"

The Ranger listened to each word Mildred Stokes said. As she finished talking an idea hit Duane with the impact of a thunderbolt. What better hiding place for a load of looted ingots than the bottom of a well? What easier spot to store them? All Murdoch would have to do was toss the bricks down a hole. No digging, no covering up, no laborious packing to some inaccessible spot.

Buck Duane, his eyes sober, rose slowly to his feet.

"What's wrong?" said Mildred Stokes.

"I'm going down the well."

"You're—what?" she gasped.

"I just got a fool notion. You'd better go into the house. I'll need to strip to my underwear."

"But you'll dirty the water," she protested. "Are you crazy?"

"I don't think so," Duane said. "We'll see."

With an incredulous glance, Mildred struggled to her feet, hurried into the cabin and firmly closed the door. Quite clearly she had decided she wanted no part in so wild an undertaking.

Duane collected his coiled rope and headed for the well. Carefully, he checked the capstan from which the wooden water bucket was lowered. It seemed solid. The handle whirled when he dropped the bucket down and he heard a splash below. Next he knotted his own rope, spacing the knots a foot or so apart. This done, he secured one end around the capstan and tossed the remainder after the bucket. Two ropes, he considered, would carry his weight without strain.

The Ranger stripped and straddled the low brick parapet, latched onto the doubled rope and began easing down, hand-over-hand.

The well was not so deep as he'd thought. Duane quickly felt the chill of water on his feet, creeping up to his knees, his thighs, his chest. After the searing heat atop the well it seemed cold, icy cold, biting into the marrow of his bones. His feet sank into soft mud.

Cautiously, water lapping around his chest, Duane quested with the toes of one foot. His pulse jumped with excitement as he explored the dark depths. The bottom of the well was studded with bricklike shapes, bedded in mud. Loosing his grip of the ropes, he drew a deep breath, ducked, fingered in sticky sediment and fastened onto one of the bricks. It came reluctantly out of the slimy ooze like a boot out of gumbo. Grasping it with both hands, Duane came erect, and stood clasping the brick to his chest, gasping.

It was as heavy as solid granite and by the faint light that filtered down through the mouth of the well he saw that it was black and slimy. Quickly, he tied it to the end of his dangling rope and dropped it, then began to climb up toward the square of bright sunlight above.

He soon discovered that while it had been a cinch dropping down, climbing was another matter. His wet fingers were numb with cold and slipped on the ropes. His arm and shoulder muscles protesting, the Ranger slowly hauled his chilled body upward.

Breathing hard, Duane struggled over the parapet, and began to haul up the brick suspended at the end of his reata. By the time he'd gotten it up, warmth was again seeping into his body.

He pulled on his pants, dug a stock knife out of a pocket, flicked the blade open, and began eagerly scraping slime off the black brick. It glinted dull yellow.

In his excitement, Duane almost ran to the cabin.

Mildred Stokes' features, plainly puzzled, were framed in a window.

"We found it!" Duane said, smiling. "The gold's at the bottom of the well."

Stunned disbelief, slowly dissolving doubt, then joy, registered in quick succession on the girl's face. She disappeared for an instant. Then the door of the cabin was flung open and the schoolma'am hurried out.

Duane handed her the brick, dripping slime. "Scrape it!" he said. "It's the only way of making sure."

Cuddling his find, Mildred Stokes hurried back into the cabin. Duane followed with his face set in tight lines. Dumping the heavy brick on the table in the leanto kitchen, Mildred Stokes reflected a knife from a shelf and began paring off sticky black scale.

"Gold!" she breathed, as shining yellow showed through.

"And there's plenty more bricks where that one came from," Duane said.

"So that's why Uncle suggested I clean out the well," exclaimed Mildred, her green eyes shining. "Oh, how dense can a person be!" She turned to Duane. "Can we salvage the others?"

He fingered his chin. "We can," he said. "After sundown. There are too many eyes in these hills to set to work now."

It was midnight before Duane quit, chilled and boneweary. Fifteen bricklike ingots, dripping black slime, were stacked beside the well. "The rest are down there," he said. "I'm sure of that now. We'll take these inside the cabin and hide them. The rest are safer where they are for the moment." Now that the excitement was wearing off, Duane felt boneweary and grateful for a needed rest.

He turned to Mildred Stokes. "You get some sleep, ma'am," he told her. "I'll carry these ingots inside and then bed down here for the rest of the night."

"Do you think I could sleep *now*?" she said.

Duane was too tired to argue. After he'd carried the ingots inside the cabin he started a fire in the stove and dried off his sodden pants. Then he wrapped himself in a couple of blankets and stretched out on the porch. While he slept, Mildred Stokes patroled restlessly from cabin to well. Not a single rifleshot disturbed the silence of the night.

With dawn Buck Duane awoke. Mildred, haggard with fatigue, sat on the porch steps.

"You need to rest!" he told her gently.

"I'll never rest until that gold is safe," she said, with a drawn smile. "I'm more grateful to you than I can say— Buck." It was the first time she had ever addressed him by his first name.

"I'll get Welch," the Ranger told her. "But first, we'd both better have some hot coffee."

Not even the prospect of a warming drink could wrench Mildred Stokes from the square pile of grimy bricks. When Duane saddled up and pulled away, he left her still hovering around the treasure.

Jogging across the valley flats, Duane thought of her keeping solitary vigil, and battled growing misgivings. It was a sure thing, he reflected, that the renegades, or CCC, maybe both, were still keeping a sharp watch on Murdoch's place. The night had been so dark he doubted that they could have seen him strip and descend the well. But still the remote possibility gnawed at him.

When the Ranger reached town, he tied up outside the law shack—and found it vacant. Emerging almost at a run, he was buttonholed by the beady-eyed Ma Purdy.

"I heard Cal Carson is withdrawing the rustling charge!" she fired at him in her flat, dry tone.

"Yes, ma'am," he said. "Have you seen Welch around?"

"Haven't seen Frosty since yesterday noon," she declared. "You still working for Miss Stokes out at Murdoch's?"

He nodded, and was relieved when she asked him no more questions. Striding up street, he met Julius Siegler.

"I've been looking for you!" the storekeeper said. "What's this I hear about your tying up with Miss Stokes? Why do you think I went your bail?"

Duane was his affable self. "Simmer down!" he advised. "I've been working on the girl. Would you pay a thousand for that quarter-section?"

"Why—why, of course," stammered Siegler, remembering Mildred Stokes had been cold to a two thousand offer.

"You tender a thousand dollars next time she comes to town, and I'm sure she'll take it," said Duane, and strode away.

Inquiries at the saloon, the barber shop, the livery, yielded no news of the town marshal. The barkeep at The Bull Pen pointed out that it wasn't uncommon for Frosty Welch to be out of town, since his bailiwack took in the entire valley and recently rustlers had been a nuisance.

Torn between anxiety for Mildred Stokes' welfare and the importance of locating the marshal, Duane fretted around town for an hour or more. Finally, he left word for

179

Welch to meet him at the Murdoch cabin. Then he headed back to the hills.

XIX

It was quiet when Buck Duane jogged into Murdoch's place—much too quiet. When Bullet rounded the cabin, his eyes sought the well. He thought Mildred Stokes might be standing guard there. She was nowhere in sight. Restraining a growing premonition, he stepped down from his horse and walked toward the cabin looking for the girl.

When he'd pulled out to go to town, something must have happened he was reluctant to let himself think about.

The sound of muffled groaning from the closed cabin spun him into action. Two quick steps took him across the porch. He threw the door open. Bound hand and foot, a bandana muffling her mouth, Mildred Stokes was writhing on the floor, baffled anger in her green eyes.

In a flash Duane was down on his knees beside her, ripping off her bonds. She came to a sitting position, ruefully rubbing her slim wrists, wealed and reddened by rawhide rope.

"That crooked marshal!" Mildred exclaimed. There was no panic in her flat tone, just bitter vexation.

"Frosty Welch—crooked?" Duane stared at her incredulously.

"Crooked as a rattlesnake," she said back, tight with anger.

"What gave you that idea?" Duane asked.

"Just after you left, he rode in with some mules," she said. "I wondered how he got out here so quickly, but before I could speak he grabbed me, wrenched my arms behind my back, tied me hand and foot. Then he bound and gagged me and dumped me in the cabin."

Duane stood frowning, trying to assimilate the girl's amazing charge. So Welch had gone bad! It seemed unbelievable. While supposedly out trailing rustlers he must have gone down into the well and made off with the gold which had not been removed. But where had he rounded up the mules? And where was he packing the loot?

There seemed to be but one answer—the Border. Mexico was the best place for a renegade lawman, where he'd be safe from posses and pursuit.

"I'm taking off," Duane told the girl quietly. "I'm going after Welch."

"You'll never catch up with him," she said, with flat hopelessness. "He's been gone for hours. And who knows where?"

"I think I know," said Duane as he headed for the door.

He filled his waterbag, hung it on the horn and started off. Hour after hour, Bullet jogged southward. The grass-carpeted valley flats lay far behind and the ragged silhouette of the Aristos had long faded into the heat haze in the rider's rear. Bullet's hooves rang upon heat-hardened earth, patched with thorny growth.

Westward, the shapes of distant ranges floated blue above the horizon, but ahead lay nothing but arid desert, its surface a monotony of cactus, sand and eroded rock. Into this, the horse plodded, a mite crawling through an infinity of space. Dust-mantled, eyes slitted against the sunglare, its rider gazed across the arid expanse, seeking some sign that his quarry lay ahead—and finding none.

Seemed, Duane considered, he was gambling on a busted flush. The terrain was strange to him. He was ignorant of its trails and waterholes. Likely he'd ride blindly ahead until his mount quit, gaunted. Meanwhile, Welch, to whom the terrain was as familiar as the palm of his hand, made his leisurely way toward the Border by another route.

Shadows lengthened as the sun dropped westward. A rattler slithered from beneath a rock, dust devils whirled across the waste, the buckskin's steady pace faltered. Duane drew rein and stepped down. He drank briefly from the sagging waterbag, spilled what remained into his hand

and held it to Bullet's dustcrusted muzzle.

Then he slacked cinches and rocked the saddle. Building a smoke, he surveyed the darkening waste around. The sun, a glowing ball of red, was sinking behind a mountain chain far to the west. A myriad of shadows patched the desert. Seemed he'd have to forget Welch, he reflected, and give all his thought to survival. Bullet was jaded, he'd used up his water, he had no more chance of recovering those ingots than a wax cat had of surviving in hell.

Across the plain, beams of the dying sun touched the tip of a finger of rock, projecting from the maw of the desert, gilding it golden. A half-forgotten memory stirred in Duane's mind. He'd once heard a puncher speak of Pinnacle Wells. Maybe he'd stumbled across the Wells. If so, it would be a life-saver, and provide a good spot to spend the night.

The stars flamed overhead when the Ranger approached the dim bulk of the pinnacle. The terrain had broken up into a jumble of sundered rock. Threading between boulders, Duane steered his weary pony toward its base. Through the night gleamed a dull red glow, pricking like an oversized cigarette tip through the darkness. A camp fire, he thought, and checked his mount. Tautly alert now, he slid out of the saddle, trailed his reins and lifted his Winchester out of the boot.

Afoot, he began scrambling ahead, worming through a chaos of heaped rock. The moon, near full, floated from behind slow-drifting masses of cottony cloud and its pale light bathed the pinnacle. Not a hundred paces from the campfire now, squirming between boulders, Duane glimpsed mules and a horse, bunched beyond the fire. Kiacks and rigging were stacked nearby, part-covered by a tarp.

Like a dark mirror, an irregular sheet of water pooled in a rocky basin, reflecting the stars. A bedroll lay spread by the fire, but there was no sign of life, beyond the animals. Luck had sure dealt aces, considered the Ranger, with surging triumph.

Cautiously, Duane crawled ahead, reached a sandy

stretch, sparcely dotted with huge fragments of talus. Suddenly a bullet screeched off a nearby rock in shrill ricochet. He flattened, the report of a Winchester ringing in his ears. Silence again enveloped the waterhole. Again, he began worming ahead. The report of a second gunshot punched into his ears. Flying grit blinded him as the slug bedded in sand, almost in his face. He cried out, as though in agony, rolled and lay sprawled behind a misshapen chunk of rock.

It was an old trick, he reflected, simulating death in order to draw an enemy out of cover, and likely it wouldn't fool an oldtimer like Frosty Welch. Anyway, from the gunflash, he'd located the source of the shooting—a nest of boulders beyond the pool.

For awhile the Range lay waiting, but the unseen marksman gave no further sign of his presence. Stealthily, Duane began to pull back, sticking to the shadows. When he figured he was beyond sight of his opponent, he began to circle, working toward the flank of the nested boulders.

Bedded down, Duane watched the boulders, silvered by moonlight. Silence shrouded the scene. He had no option but to wait it out, he decided—either until the marshal became convinced he had tagged his pursuer and emerged from cover, or day dawned. Daylight should give him an edge.

Time dragged. A meteor flashed across the sky, and was consumed. Feathery talus dust floated down from the pinnacle towering above like fine rain. A hoof clicked on rock as a mule changed position.

Stretched out behind cover, Duane fought an overwhelming urge to sleep. He'd been in the saddle since sunup. He was bone-weary, and his eyelids seemed loaded with lead. Once or twice, he snapped up his drooping head.

Drowsily, he became aware that dawn was breaking. The mules, the ashes of the dead fire, and the stacked gear took shape through wan gray light. Overhead, the heavens began to lighten and the stars to dim. Suddenly, like a jack-in-the-box, a man's head and shoulders showed above the clutter of boulders. Duane shook off his drowsiness, cuddled the Winchester to a shoulder. Tensed, with his finger hooked on the trigger, he lay watching.

For a full minute, the marshal stood unmoving, except for his head as it swiveled while he searched the shadows. Then, his rifle slanted under one arm, he stepped out into the open.

Duane called out the marshal's name. The renegade lawman pivoted, quick as a teased cat, and swung up the barrel of his Winchester. Duane's rifle barked just once. Welch jackknifed, dropping the Winchester, clutching at his stomach. Bunched up, he fell forward, lay twisting spasmodically.

Muscles cramped, Duane came slowly to his feet, moved cautiously toward the wounded man, his rifle leveled. Closing up, he saw there was no fight left in the gasping, squirming lawman. He kicked the rifle out of reach, bent and slid Welch's sixgun out of its holster and placed it beneath his own waistband. Blood, bright scarlet, seeped around the marshal's belt buckle.

"You played out of luck, Frosty," Duane said, eying the twisting form.

Welch rolled onto his back, knees doubled up. "Did you have to tag me in the guts?" he gasped.

Duane said nothing, hunkering beside the mortally wounded man.

"A smoke!" begged the marshal.

Duane rolled a cigarette, placed it between the dying man's lips and touched a match to the tip. In a spasm of agony, Welch bit it off. Duane flicked the glowing end into the sand.

The marshal lay tensed, thin lips compressed, fingers digging into his stomach, bleak eyes fastened on Duane.

"You fooled me," he muttered hoarsely. "Figured I'd tagged you with that second shot." His eroded features twisted into a humorless grin, "Well, I almost made it!"

Duane fashioned a smoke for himself. "So you saw a chance and took it!"

"Chance! Hell, I organized the hold-up, figured it out

with Murdoch, and cut three hardcases in to lend a hand."

Duane looked reflectively at the dying lawman. Carefully the Ranger reached for the other's rifle, squeezed trigger, ejected the empty and eyed its base. "Murdoch crossed you, and you fed him two slugs, with this Winchester," he said.

"It was a pleasure!"

Then your hardcases got busy digging," said Duane. "How is it they're not around?"

"I sent them on ahead, to San Pereto across the Border, to wait for their cut."

"So you were heading for San Pereto?"

Welch's teeth locked against pain, then he returned hoarsely, "Nope—El Quito."

"Isn't that pueblo forty miles east of San Pereto?"

"Sure!" Cold humor sparked in the marshal's pale eyes. "I just didn't figure on a divvy."

"You sure are a prime double-crosser," said Duane with disgust.

He rose, sauntered over to the stacked gear. As he expected, the mules' kiacks were heavy with the black bricks. Welch, he considered, would never survive the ride back to Hertzburg. At the most, he'd never last more than three days—three days of agony. Returning to the wounded man, the Ranger stood looking down at him.

"I'm going to leave you, and bring back a doctor," he said. "You'd never survive the ride back to town."

Another spasm of pain contorted Welch's thin features. "No sawbones can help me—not with a slug in my belly," he whispered hoarsely. "You just leave my sixgun."

Duane lifted the Colt from beneath his waistband, set it carefully beside the doomed man and backed away, hand on the butt of his own ivory-butted .45. Welch, he reflected, was no more to be trusted than a dying rattlesnake.

Out of range, the Ranger began to pick his way between scattered rock toward his saddlehorse.

The deep boom of a .45 reverberated in his ears.

XX

Then Buck Duane came riding into San Antonio for the second time in—How long had it been actually? Two decades, a century and a half? He no longer felt like a stranger to himself. He would feel that way again before long, he was sure of that. But now at least he felt like a whole man, complete in every aspect of himself.

The dark stranger would always be with him, the killer from his ancestral past. But he had drawn that killer's claws this time with a vengeance, for though he had been fast on the trigger and brought a scheming, hypocritical scoundrel to justice, he had felt, even as his gun flamed and roared that it was a Texas Ranger who was doing the shooting, and not an ancestral ghost skulking in shadows with his passion for slaying out of control.

Duane wondered just what MacNelly was going to say to him. Though he had received a telegram of congratulation a few hours after he'd wired his superior a full report, nothing could take the place of a face-to-face meeting.

Duane didn't think MacNelly was going to pin medals on him. But he was looking forward to a reception that would cheer and warm him a little, and give him a justified feeling of pride.

Ten minutes after he'd entered the outskirts of town Duane was tying Bullet to a hitching rack in front of the Buckhorn Hotel where he'd had his previous talk with the Captain. Then in a few minutes Buck Duane was shaking hands with MacNelly. The two dilapidated rocking chairs were at his back, standing in almost the same place where the earlier chairs had been.

MacNelly had risen instantly on catching sight of Duane. The Captain's handclasp was warm and firm.

Then they both sat down and Duane waited for the man-to-man congratulations to come pouring out of the Captain. Instead, MacNelly took two telegrams out of his pocket and handed them to Duane without saying a word.

The Ranger tore the first one open and read: "Tell Mr.

Duane all is forgiven. Tell him, please, that I will be waiting for him to tell me that he was very foolish to threaten to put me across his knee and spank me as if I were a little girl. I am not a little girl. Tell him, please, that I am waiting to prove to him that I am a woman." It was signed—"Rosita."

The second one he read with just as much astonishment. "I feel that it is my duty to inform you that Mr. Duane has performed the task assigned to him with exemplary courage and single-minded dedication. Please assure him that I will never cease to be grateful to him." It was signed "Mildred Stokes."

"You're quite a hand with the women, aren't you?" MacNelly said, looking at him with a broad grin on his face.

"A Ranger has to be able to deal with anything that comes up," Duane said solemnly, "bad men, wild cards, and good women. And I'm not saying which is the most trouble!"

ZANE GREY

LAST OF
THE DUANES

Buck Duane's father was a gunfighter who died by the gun, and, in accepting a drunken bully's challenge, Duane finds himself forced into the life of an outlaw. He roams the dark trails of southwestern Texas, living in outlaw camps, until he meets the one woman who can help him overcome his past—a girl named Jennie Lee.

___4430-7 $4.99 US/$5.99 CAN

Dorchester Publishing Co., Inc.
P.O. Box 6640
Wayne, PA 19087-8640

Please add $1.75 for shipping and handling for the first book and $.50 for each book thereafter. NY, NYC, and PA residents, please add appropriate sales tax. No cash, stamps, or C.O.D.s. All orders shipped within 6 weeks via postal service book rate. Canadian orders require $2.00 extra postage and must be paid in U.S. dollars through a U.S. banking facility.

Name_____
Address_____
City_____ State_____ Zip_____
I have enclosed $_____ in payment for the checked book(s).
Payment <u>must</u> accompany all orders. ❑ Please send a free catalog.
    CHECK OUT OUR WEBSITE! www.dorchesterpub.com

TIMBAL GULCH TRAIL

"Brand is a topnotcher!"
—New York Times

Les Burchard owns the local gambling palace, half the town, and most of the surrounding territory, and Walt Devon's thousand-acre ranch will make him king of the land. The trouble is, Devon doesn't want to sell. In a ruthless bid to claim the spread, Burchard tries everything from poker to murder. But Walt Devon is a betting man by nature, even when the stakes are his life. The way Devon figures, the odds are stacked against him, so he can either die alone or take his enemy to the grave with him.

_3828-5 $4.50 US/$5.50 CAN

DAN'L BOONE

DODGE TYLER

THE KAINTUCKS

The Natchez Trace is the trail of choice for frontiersmen heading north from New Orleans. But for Dan'l Boone and his small band of boatmen, the trail leads straight into danger. Lying in wait for the legendary guide is a band of French land pirates out for the payroll he is protecting. And with the cutthroats is a vicious war party of Chickasaw braves out for much more—Dan'l Boone's blood!

___4466-8 $3.99 US/$4.99 CAN

Dorchester Publishing Co., Inc.
P.O. Box 6640
Wayne, PA 19087-8640

Please add $1.75 for shipping and handling for the first book and $.50 for each book thereafter. NY, NYC, and PA residents, please add appropriate sales tax. No cash, stamps, or C.O.D.s. All orders shipped within 6 weeks via postal service book rate. Canadian orders require $2.00 extra postage and must be paid in U.S. dollars through a U.S. banking facility.

Name_____

Address_____

City_____State_____Zip_____

I have enclosed $_____ in payment for the checked book(s).

Payment <u>must</u> accompany all orders. ❑ Please send a free catalog.

BLOOD HUNT

David Thompson

With only his oldest friend and his trusty long rifle for company, Davy Crockett explores the wild frontier looking for adventure, and has the strength and cunning to face any enemy. But even he may have met his match when he gets caught between two warring tribes on one side and a dangerous band of white men on the other—all of them willing to die—and kill—for a group of stolen women. It is up to Crockett to save the women, his friend and his own hide if he wants to live to explore another day.

_4229-0 $3.99 US/$4.99 CAN

Dorchester Publishing Co., Inc.
P.O. Box 6640
Wayne, PA 19087-8640

Please add $1.75 for shipping and handling for the first book and $.50 for each book thereafter. NY, NYC, and PA residents, please add appropriate sales tax. No cash, stamps, or C.O.D.s. All orders shipped within 6 weeks via postal service book rate. Canadian orders require $2.00 extra postage and must be paid in U.S. dollars through a U.S. banking facility.

Name_____
Address_____
City_____State_____Zip_____
I have enclosed $_____ in payment for the checked book(s).
Payment <u>must</u> accompany all orders. ❑ Please send a free catalog.